CLIFFTOPPERS

THE THORN ISLAND ADVENTURE

CLIFFTOPPERS

Have you read?

THE ARROWHEAD MOOR ADVENTURE

THE FIRE BAY ADVENTURE

CLIFFTOPPERS

THE THORN ISLAND ADVENTURE

FLEUR HITCHCOCK

First published in the UK in 2020 by Nosy Crow Ltd
The Crow's Nest, 14 Baden Place
Crosby Row, London SE1 1YW, UK

Nosy Crow and associated logos are trademarks and/or registered trademarks of Nosy Crow Ltd

1 3 5 7 9 10 8 6 4 2

A CIP catalogue record for this book is available from the British Library.

Printed and bound in Great Britain by Clays Ltd, Elcograf S.p.A.
Typeset by Tiger Media

Papers used by Nosy Crow are made from wood grown in sustainable forests.

ISBN: 978 1 78800 790 0

www.nosycrow.com

For Mum and our long holiday

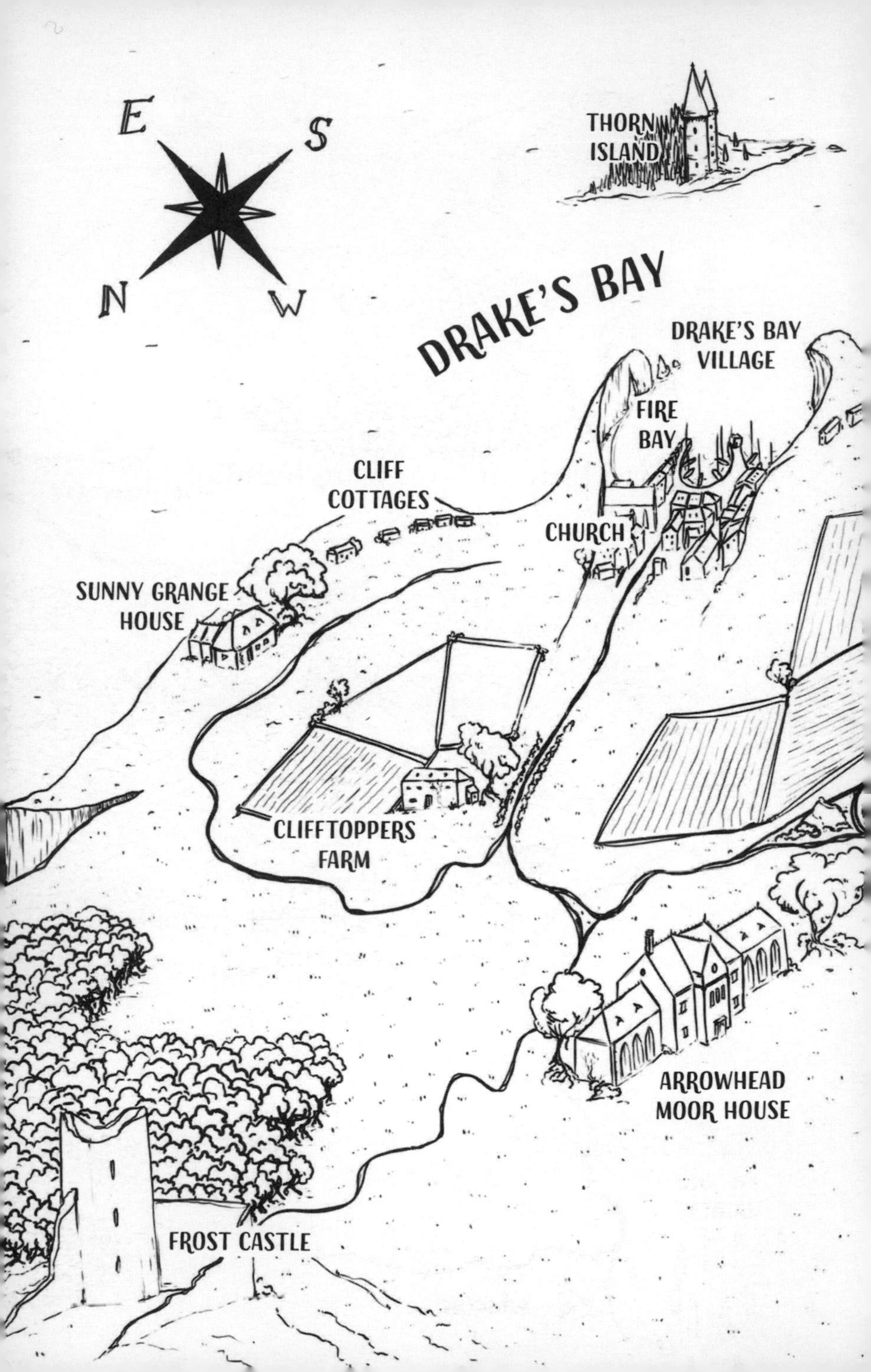
E
S
N
W
THORN ISLAND
DRAKE'S BAY
DRAKE'S BAY VILLAGE
FIRE BAY
CLIFF COTTAGES
CHURCH
SUNNY GRANGE HOUSE
CLIFFTOPPERS FARM
ARROWHEAD MOOR HOUSE
FROST CASTLE

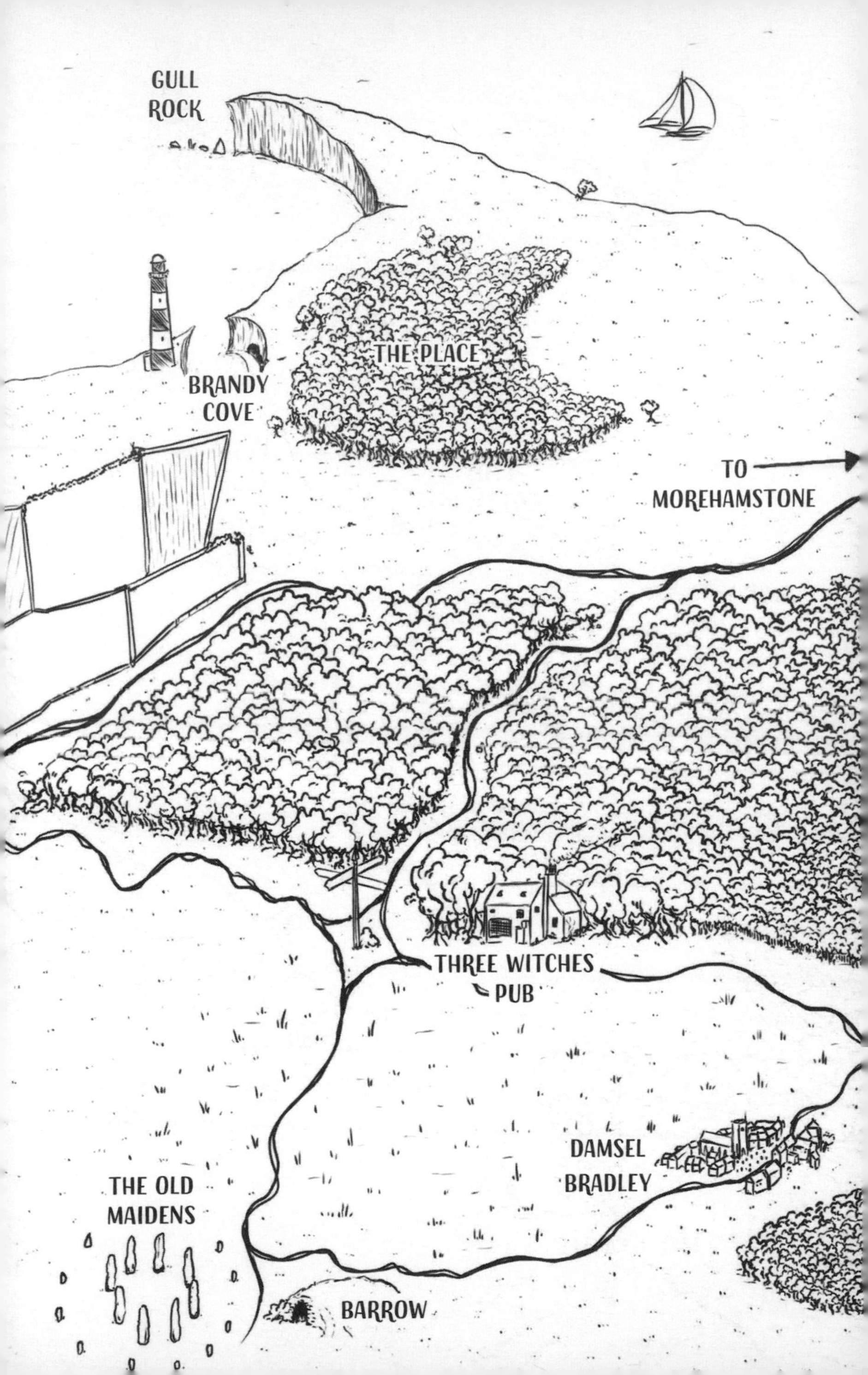
GULL ROCK
BRANDY COVE
THE PLACE
TO MOREHAMSTONE
THREE WITCHES PUB
DAMSEL BRADLEY
THE OLD MAIDENS
BARROW

CHAPTER 1

Eight-year-old Josh lay with his red notebook on a low wall, spying on the village shop. So far one person had gone in and come out again holding a pint of milk. He wasn't on to any mysteries yet, but it was only nine o'clock.

He had high hopes – after all, every time they came to stay with their grandparents at Clifftopper Farm something happened. Something much more exciting than any of the things that happened at home.

Above him two seagulls circled. In the distance

a trawler chugged through Drake's Bay, more seagulls following. Sunlight sparkled on the water and warmed his back. Rigging slapped gently against the yacht masts. It all sounded summery, relaxed, happy. For a moment he forgot that he was looking for excitement, and just enjoyed the warmth and the freedom.

Bella, his grandparents' dog, stretched herself next to him on the hot stones and stared out to sea. "Feels good, doesn't it, Bella," he said, sliding his fingers into the curls of her coat. Bella groaned in agreement.

He heard the screech of a bike and turned to see his cousin Chloe arrive. She shook her hair out from her bike helmet and breathed in the fresh sea breeze. "Grandma said the Plaice and Ships's got a new owner – have you seen anyone yet?"

Josh shuffled around ninety degrees so that he got a good view of the café to his right.

Not that there was anything to see. Eight chairs and two tables.

An ice-cream sign flapping in the breeze.

Then, as he watched, a man came out of the door, wiped a dirty cloth over one of the tables and went back inside.

Josh pulled his notebook from his shorts and wrote: *Not very clean but no visible signs of criminal behaviour.*

"Of course I'm sure!" someone bellowed. "It's not a mistake!"

Chloe scrambled on to the wall to see better.

"Where's it coming from?" Josh asked.

Chloe pointed towards the quay steps by the harbour master's office where a tall man in faded denims – Jake, a local fisherman – looked red and angry.

"It was there one minute and gone the next! Someone saw it! They must have done!"

Beside him the harbour master shook his head and said something Josh couldn't hear.

"But it's brand new…"

A family, crabbing on the quay, edged away, moving their buckets and lines out of Jake's way.

"C'mon," said Josh, striding across the tarmac. He heard Chloe jump down from the wall behind him. The closer they got, the more he could hear and it was clear that Jake had lost something important.

"It has to have been stolen," he said. "It just has to have been."

"Here, Jake, I'll get the shortwave radio going. Call the police," said the harbour master. "Where's it gone from?"

Jake pointed towards the lighthouse cliff, and stomped into the office with the harbour master.

The cousins paused at the top of the quay steps, staring in the direction Jake had pointed in. There was sea, and cliff, and seagulls. No boat. No thieves. It all looked picture-postcard calm.

Seconds later, Jake's voice rang out from the office. "Two minutes!" he said. "Two flippin' minutes parked up on the shingle round in Brandy Cove and it only goes and disappears. I only got back here because of a tourist in a rowing boat… Yes – an hour ago!"

Chloe and Josh stood just outside the harbour master's office, listening. It was a large shed with peeling green paint and more things inside than could possibly fit. Jake was sitting at the paper-strewn desk talking into an ancient telephone receiver. Mobile phones were unreliable in Drake's Bay. In fact, they didn't really work anywhere on the Dragon Peninsula, so the harbour master's office acted like an emergency call box.

"Yes – I was in the cave mending the lobster pots; turned round and it had gone!" Jake rubbed his face. He'd changed from boiling red to disturbingly white.

"It's cream, with a blue cabin. It's called the *Mermaid*. And it's brand new," he said, his voice wobbling. "Can't fish without it. It's my livelihood."

"Stolen?" asked Josh, but nobody listened.

The harbour master brushed past Josh to fill his kettle from the outside tap.

"Tomorrow!" said Jake. "It'll be halfway to nowhere by then. How come there's no police today?" Jake went quiet and then let out a sigh. "Oh – yes, I can see that might be more important. OK, tomorrow it is then."

Chloe turned at the sound of bicycles. It was Ava, Josh's older sister, and their cousin, Aiden.

"Boat shed," called Aiden, tilting his head, and Chloe, Josh and Bella charged across the harbour, Josh bursting with the news.

"Guess what?" shouted Josh, running. "It's gone – vanished! Can we try to find it with the *Black*

Diamond, sis?" said Josh. "Please?"

"Find what with the *Black Diamond*?" asked Ava, leaning her bike against a small timbered building.

"It's cream and blue," said Josh. "It's disappeared and the police can't come until tomorrow."

"I nearly got killed by a man in a van," said Ava. "In case you're interested."

"She did," said Aiden.

"So if we took the *Black Diamond*," continued Josh, "we could get to the bay and have a look for clues and maybe find it before they even come."

"Couldn't we just mess about on the boat and eat sandwiches?" suggested Chloe quietly.

Ava shook her head. "Seriously, Josh? What are you even talking about?"

A moment later, Ava unlocked the back door of the boat shed where Grandpa Edward's precious boat, the *Black Diamond*, was moored.

"So this white van nearly knocked us off the road. I thought he was going to hit Ava," said Aiden, gesticulating with the sandwich bag so enthusiastically that he nearly sent Josh into the water. "He was going really fast. And then he stopped and asked us the way to the lighthouse. Like he'd never nearly killed us."

"I ended up in the hedge," said Ava, checking the weal on her calf from the bramble thorns. "Awesome dog, though."

"Beautiful Dalmatian," agreed Aiden. "Oh, Mrs Murphy – hello."

"Morning dears, taking the *Black Diamond* out?" asked a smiley lady with very sparkly spectacles. She stuck her head round the door of the shed and into the middle of the conversation. "Your grandparents are very trusting. You're only ten, aren't you, Ava?"

"Twelve," corrected Ada.

"And I'm eleven," said Aiden.

"And I'm nine," said Chloe, reassembling the sandwiches.

"And I'm—" started Josh.

"Yes, yes, well, while you're out there," interrupted Mrs Murphy, "see if you can find Jake Marley's boat." She tapped the side of her nose, as if she knew something they didn't.

"Oh yes, we saw Jake. He was really mad. He said '*I was in the cave mending the lobster pots; turned round and it had gone*'," said Josh, reading from his notebook.

"We're off to look for it," said Aiden.

Mrs Murphy's disappointment was almost invisible, but she shuffled slightly as if to make herself bigger and sniffed. "Well, you know all about it then." She glanced down at the newspaper in her bag. "But," she said, her eyes brightening, "do you know about the Charlie's Cheerful Chews thing?" She gazed gleefully at their blank faces.

"What's that?" asked Chloe.

"Oh – well!" Mrs Murphy settled her bottom against the doorframe as if she was there for a long chat. "So, you've all heard of Charlie's Cheerful Chews?"

Aiden nodded. "Seen the adverts, yeah."

"Well, Charlie Constantinides of Charlie's Cheerful Chews, you know, the dog treats, has a son, a little chap, George, only six..." Mrs Murphy searched the air for inspiration. "Anyway, he's been kidnapped – and they've asked for an enormous ransom." She pulled a very grave face and waited for their reaction.

"Where's he been taken from?" asked Ava.

"When?" asked Josh.

"How?" asked Aiden.

Mrs Murphy kept up the serious face. "Oh, it's quite awful – I don't know anything really. Almost nothing. No more than he lives in Little Chaffering. You know, that ridiculous great house about ten miles inland. Frightfully rich, you know. And that his poor parents are desperate. Anyway –" she flashed a smile – "I'm off to have my hair done. Bye." With that she waddled away from the boat shed, making her way uphill towards the tiny high street.

CHAPTER 2

Ava took the tiller of the *Black Diamond* and pushed away from the jetty. The boat slid into the calm waters of the harbour. For Ava, sailing the boat was probably the best thing in the entire world and when, last year, Grandpa had declared her a good enough sailor to captain the dinghy alone, Ava had done handstands across the kitchen, she was so happy. Now she felt the wind pick up. It caught her braids and whipped the mainsail, and she knew they'd be able to get along the coast quite comfortably.

Beside her Chloe sat very still, wearing a life jacket and looking a little green.

"You'll get over it," smiled Ava.

"I know – it's just I always feel a bit sick on the boat." Chloe turned towards the wind, and Ava noticed that her younger cousin was gripping the side and that her knuckles had turned white.

Josh sat on the bow, whooping and trailing a crab weight in the water. "I can see right into the sea!" he shouted. "Billions of fish."

"If you fall in, I'm not rescuing you," shouted his sister. Bella joined in, barking at Josh until he sat back in the boat. "See," laughed Ava. "Bella agrees."

Just inside the bow, Aiden had one of Grandpa's coastal maps unfolded on his lap and barely seemed to notice that they had set sail.

She didn't actually need him to find the beach on the map; she knew which one they were heading for. It was small, and if she pulled up the centreboard that stuck through the bottom of the dinghy, they should be able to get quite close to shore. Especially now that the tide was in. After all, Jake had managed to get his boat on to the beach and it must have been much bigger and heavier than the *Black Diamond*, which was large for a dinghy but didn't have a proper cabin.

Steering her way round a flotilla of sea kayaks she headed out of the harbour into the open bay. "Ready about!" she shouted.

"Lee ho!" replied Chloe as she ducked under the boom and sat on the high side of the boat, helping to balance it, her hair catching in the wind and looking very nearly like a proper sailor.

Ava pulled in the rope controlling the mainsail, feeling it strain against her fingers as it swept the *Black Diamond* across the bay, the prow bounding over the surface of the water. The feeling was like nothing else in the world – better than running, better than cycling. Even better than swimming.

"Round to thc right," shouted Aiden.

"Starboard, you idiot," shouted Josh.

"He knows," said Ava. "It's just that he doesn't have to show that he knows – unlike some people."

Ignoring her, Josh dangled his hand over the side of the boat, tipping the *Black Diamond* the wrong way.

"Hey," the other three shouted, and he sat back

up, but not before Bella went and sat by him, resting her head on his knee. Like a guard.

Upright, the *Black Diamond* cut through the water, and they struck out to sea towards Thorn Island, which lay like a green jewel in the middle of Drake's Bay. Ava swung the boat round when they could clearly see the faces of the tourists disembarking from the little ferry, and tacked back inland across the football pitch of open water between the island and the shore. From out here Brandy Cove was easy to identify. It had tall yellow cliffs behind it, the lighthouse at the top and the dark holes of caves below. Ava held the tiller steady and let the boat race as fast as she would go.

Looking up from the map, Aiden took a pair of binoculars from the forward locker and studied the cliffs and the lighthouse in search of the man or the Dalmatian. He could just make out the caves at Brandy Cove, but nothing more. He put down the binoculars and stared into the deep blue water rushing past the boat.

Somehow he felt the stolen boat and the rude man in the van with the dog had to be connected. But he couldn't see how.

It was just that the van had been on its way to the lighthouse, which was at the top of the cliff, and the boat had been at the bottom.

He shook his head and gazed across the waves, and soon his mind turned to swimming. The water was so clear. So tempting.

Ava guided the *Black Diamond* straight towards the shore, the boat slowing as the wind dropped, and they slid to a gentle halt a metre from where the shingle rose from the water. There were no boats in the cove. No people. It was utterly deserted.

"How deep do you reckon it is?" asked Aiden.

"I'll find out," said Chloe, lowering her bare feet into the water. The sea stopped just below her shorts. "Cold!" she giggled, glad to be on solid ground.

"Pull us in, please, Chloe," said Ava.

Chloe waded round to the front of the boat and tugged on the painter. The *Black Diamond* obediently floated on to the beach until her bow rested on the shingle. Josh leaped off, splashing everyone but managing to stay quite dry. Ava followed, while Aiden stayed on the boat, peering at the map. Bella stood on the bow watching and then sprang straight on to the pebbles and into the nearest cave of which there were six: five small and one huge, all of them very dark and probably very interesting if you were a dog.

They looked around for clues. But there was no sign of Jake's boat. No sign of it ever having been there. No sign of it having been dragged out to sea.

Chloe looked up at the cliffs. "Well, it didn't go up there," she said.

"And it didn't go in here," said Josh, staggering out of the nearest cave, his fingers pinching his nose and making exaggerated sick gestures. "Urgh. Stinks. Bella – how can you stand it?"

"What of?" asked Ava.

"Crab bottoms," said Josh, stumbling over to stand at the bottom of the cliff. "Hey – what about that path? Could have gone up there."

"Get real, Josh, you couldn't take a boat up a path," said Ava, stomping away towards the *Black Diamond*.

"Why not?" said Josh.

Ava ignored him.

Chloe was checking out the other caves. The high tide had left plastic and wood on the rocky walls of the first one and the remains of something dead and feathered on the floor. "Yuck!" she said.

She tried the next cave, which was empty but for nets, and the next, the largest, which had some coiled rope, but there was no brand-new fishing boat hidden inside. "Nothing," she said to the dripping walls.

She came out to find Ava clambering back on the boat, and Josh trying to climb up a vertical cliff face.

"What are you doing?" she asked.

"Checking that the boat isn't up here," he said.

Chloe shook her head and lifted her leg over the side of the boat. "Your turn to do the pushing."

"You're all boring," said Josh, giving the boat a shove and then leaping into the stern.

"Josh, it is absolutely obvious that you couldn't drag an enormous great boat up a cliff. I mean you couldn't. Chloe's right," said Ava again, swinging the *Black Diamond* back out to face Thorn Island. "It's got to be somewhere along the coast."

"Yeah, but no one saw it. Perhaps they've got some brilliant machine that would haul it up on to the cliff and then vanish it." Josh stood up, banging his head on the boom and rocking the boat from side to side.

"Er, yes," said Aiden. "Back to reality: the boat could easily be hidden in any of these fingery bits along the island," he said, pointing at the map.

"Yup," said Ava. "Exactly."

Josh mouthed something and looked purposefully into the sea as they sped back over towards the island.

Ava brought the *Black Diamond* close to the shore, and they glided past, peering into tiny bays and round wooded islets.

The sun grew warm and then hot on their backs, and still they combed the coast. Ava pulled out a tube of sun cream, offering it to the others and coating her arms with the white gloop and rubbing it in until it disappeared and her arms were shiny brown. She squeezed some on Josh who squealed and wriggled and tried to wash it off, but instead it left oily rainbows on the sea.

Aiden handed out the picnic.

Chloe leaned against the funny old cushions that smelled of creosote and weedkiller and ate her sandwich. Her head rested in the bow so that she looked up at the sky.

Egg. Egg and cress. Grandpa hadn't forgotten that she was a vegetarian. She took a big bite and sat up to stop herself choking. Past the sail she had a clear view of one of the follies built in the grounds of Thorn House. The sun was on it, picking out the ivy that crept up the tower. It looked so romantic. Chloe daydreamed while she munched and stared. A Rapunzel tower. Definitely in need of a maiden with really long hair probably knitting straw and waiting to be rescued. And then something caught her eye, up at the tiny pointed window at the top of the tower. A white face with a round screaming mouth shouting at her through the glass.

She dropped her sandwich into the water.

CHAPTER 3

"I did see someone," said Chloe, pushing her bike over the piles of nets on the quay. "I'm absolutely sure of it."

"I think it was a reflection," said Aiden.

"Or a ghost? Whoooo!" said Josh, taking his hands off the handlebars and waving his arms over his head.

"Josh," warned Ava.

"Well, it *is* haunted, isn't it?" Josh replied. "I mean, don't the ghosts wander up and down? You know, scaring people and whoooooing. Like in *The*

Pirates of the Caribbean?"

Ava's mouth twitched. "Sorry, but there was nothing the second time we passed."

"I know no one else saw anything," said Chloe, "but I am sure. I'd sort of like to tell the police." She walked on, almost talking to herself, "but they couldn't help Jake and his boat's been stolen. They said to him that they couldn't come until tomorrow." She clapped her hand to her mouth and swung round to face the others. "Oh! They're looking for that child. Perhaps that's who I saw."

"The Charlie's Cheerful Chews child?" said Josh, launching into the advert. "*Charlie, Charlie, love your dooooooooog!*" He leaned down to kiss Bella who barked at him and sneezed him away.

"Seriously?" said Ava. "On an island? Here? No – I don't think so."

"I still want to tell the police," said Chloe, her lower lip jutting just a little. She stomped over to the red call box next to the Plaice and Ships. Before she even opened the door she could read the sign, OUT OF ORDER, taped over the buttons. "Urgh," she said.

Aiden wrinkled up his face, as if thinking about

Chloe's idea and deciding that it was bonkers, but trying to be sympathetic all the same. "You could tell the harbour master? He could call the police."

Chloe let out a long sigh. It was obvious that no one believed her. "Will someone come with me?" she asked, feeling mildly cross and doubly sure of what she'd seen, and also convinced about the face in the window being the kidnapped child. "He can be a bit…"

"OK," said Ava. "Hold my bike," she told Josh, letting go of the handlebars and joining Chloe.

"Stop telling me what to do!" Josh shouted, but he grabbed the bike all the same.

Chloe knocked on the door of the harbour master's shed.

She knocked again.

"Hello!" Ava shouted, peering through the small window into the mass of everything nautical jammed inside the tiny space. "No one there," she said.

"He's gone to the dentist," said Pearl, the woman who rented out kayaks from the other side of the harbour. "Broke a tooth. Won't be back for ages."

"Oh!" said Chloe, almost stamping her foot. "Have you got a phone that works, please, Pearl?"

"Not down here. Hey – other way!" Pearl shouted, catching sight of one of her kayaks heading towards Thorn Island. She ran off to shout and gesticulate and send them round towards Fire Point.

"Well, that went well," said Aiden when the girls rejoined him and Josh and the bikes.

"Perhaps it wasn't there; perhaps Chloe made it up," said Josh.

"I did not!" said Chloe. She felt … cross. Actually, properly angry. She glanced over at Ava, who was taking a selfie against the calm blue sea. They were all … not taking it seriously.

"Does anyone else want a pasty?" asked Aiden.

"Go on then," said Josh, and the boys wandered over to the café.

Chloe fumed.

In the wall of the Plaice and Ships café was a little hatch, and behind the hatch stood a man in a flowery apron with a bobble hat on his head. Leaning against the wall was another man, holding a piece of an outboard motor engine. Josh paused and took out his red notebook. *Outboard motor engine in pieces. SUSPICIOUS. Very.*

"Afternoon, boys, what can I do you for?" said Mr Bobble Hat.

"Two steak pasties, please," said Aiden.

The man shook his head. "Sorry, haven't got any today," he said. "Clean out."

Aiden looked at the board. Josh pointed to the second item on the menu. "Oh, um, two chicken then?"

"No chicken ones either," said the man. "All gone."

"What have you got?" asked Josh.

The outboard-motor man wandered away to the quayside.

"Ice cream," said Mr Bobble Hat, staring over their heads. "Salted caramel or rum and raisin – what do you fancy?" Aiden looked back to where the man was looking. The girls were standing together in the middle of the paving, arguing.

"What's up with her?" asked Mr Bobble Hat, pointing at Chloe, who looked completely furious and was waving her arms about.

"Oh, she tried to get the harbour master to radio the police," said Aiden, "but he wasn't there, and the mobiles don't work and the call box is out of order."

"Oh aye," said Mr Bobble Hat. "Hopeless down here, isn't it?"

"Yes," said Aiden, warming to the man despite the lack of pasties and the lack of ice-cream flavours. "One caramel please."

"What was it about – had a bike stolen?"

"And one rum and raisin," said Josh, looking faintly disgusted. "Actually, no – caramel for me too. She thought she saw something. Someone in trouble."

"Where?"

"In the little tower on the island," said Josh.

"Oh!" said the man, turning away to wash his ice-cream scoop. "Ice creams coming up, and, tell you what, I'll ring the police for you from my landline."

The ice creams arrived and Josh called the girls over. Chloe told the man what she'd seen and he came back to the hatch, the phone in his hand. He prodded the buttons and then began to talk.

"Yes, two young ladies and two young gentlemen saw a face in the tower on Thorn Island." The man stopped and listened. "Yes, they're with me now. Can you describe the face, miss?" he asked Chloe.

She shook her head. "I only saw that it was a person shouting. I thought it might have been a child. I thought it might have been the Charlie's Cheerful Chews boy, you know."

The man repeated what she'd said and wandered back into the café, holding his hand out to the cousins so that they waited by the hatch.

A moment later, he was back.

"Very interesting, they said. AND they said to go home, not to worry about it and they'd be there very soon to investigate. Well done." Mr Bobble Hat beamed at them. "I need to close up now, but before I do would you two girls like an ice cream on the house?"

CHAPTER 4

As they approached the farm delicious baking smells wafted across the fields.

"Scones," Chloe heard Josh say. "Scones."

"Cream tea?" asked Grandpa as they ran from the bike shed back through the orchard to the farmhouse. "Primrose is just taking scones out of the oven."

Chloe followed the others; they'd obviously forgotten all about the strange face at windows and the missing boat as they crammed round the kitchen table, the aroma of baking and fresh jam filling the air. But she hadn't. She didn't feel at all as if it was over, and it was hard to sit there eating cream and jam with a head full of doubts.

"Jam and then cream," said Aiden, slicing open a scone, the heat making his glasses steam up. "It makes more sense. The jam sinks into the scone and then the cream blobs on top."

"No!" cried Josh, cracking open his second scone and slapping cream on first. "You're wrong – it has to be this way." His dollop of cream melded with the hot scone and he placed a gentle dab of jam in the centre before stuffing the whole thing into his mouth in one go. "Delishus!"

"I'm not even joking, Josh – you are soooo greedy." Ava leaned over her brother and helped herself to another scone. "Grandpa, does anyone live up at the lighthouse?"

Grandpa topped up his teacup and frowned. "I don't think so. I think it's automatic now and the buildings are closed up – why?"

"Oh, nothing," said Ava, glancing at Aiden. "Just wondered."

A silence grew and Grandpa broke it by asking, "So, what have you all been doing today, apart from building up an appetite?"

"Did you know Jake had his boat stolen? We went to look for it in the *Black Diamond*," said Ava. "Went to Brandy Cove – checked Thorn Island. Didn't find it."

"And Chloe thought she saw someone imprisoned in the little tower on the island – but it was rubbish," said Josh.

"Goodness," said Grandma. "Really?"

Chloe sighed. "Well, yes, and we got the man in the café to call the police in case it's…" She trailed off.

Grandma was shaking her head. "You're thinking about that boy that's been kidnapped, but I can tell you that they're looking in the London area – not around here. No one would ever hide a child somewhere so touristy, would they?" She rose from the table.

"See," said Josh. "You're making it up, Chloe."

Chloe kicked him under the table but had a sudden thought. "Can we borrow your binoculars?" she asked Grandma. "Please?"

"Of course," said Grandma Primrose. "I didn't know you were interested in birdwatching, Chloe dear? I always thought that was Aiden."

Chloe shrugged. "I thought I'd give it a try – I thought I saw –" Chloe struggled to remember a bird's name – "a nesting egret on the estuary."

"Really?" said Grandma. "Very late in the year – but do use them; they're on the dresser."

"What are we doing?" asked Josh. "Are we just following Chloe?"

As the golden evening light flooded the farmyard Chloe led the way to the field behind the farm. From up here there was a terrific view of Drake's Bay, Thorn Island and the lighthouse. Big round bales of straw were dotted through the stubble, leaving long shadows, and she clambered on top of a double one.

"Er, yes, what are we doing?" said Aiden, pulling himself up and reaching down to help Bella.

"Tell you in a minute," said Chloe, peering out to sea.

"You said birdwatching? Why are we looking at birds?" asked Josh, jumping off the bale and scrambling over another one. "Are we looking for the boat from up here or what?" He reached the top, punched at the air, missed his footing and fell over the far side. No one seemed to notice, so he clambered up again.

It was dead still out there. A couple of fishing boats visiting their lobster pots out at sea, a yacht stranded by the tide on the far side of the island, and families crabbing in the mud by the harbour. A perfect summer's evening.

Chloe trained the lenses on the tower. "It's just…"

"What?" asked Josh impatiently. "You're not looking at that stupid tower, are you? You heard what Grandma said."

"I don't think… I can't— Oh! What's that? There – look!" She handed the binoculars to Ava.

"What am I looking at?"

"The tower, not the window in front but the one to the right, facing the cliffs, see? There's definitely something in the window this time." Chloe turned to the others. "That means that if there was someone, and there definitely was, they haven't been rescued. The police haven't been. And I'm right, Josh – you owe me an apology."

Slowly Ava scanned Thorn Island. "I dunno," she said, handing the binoculars to Aiden.

It took Aiden a second to find the window. "I can see…" he said. "But it's definitely not a face." He fiddled with the focus. "It's like writing on the glass, and then maybe someone behind. Waving? Although it's kind of white – and— Oh, I don't know … there might be nothing at all."

"Let me have a go," said Josh, hauling himself up to the top of the bale and sitting on Ava's feet before yanking the binoculars out of her hands.

"Josh!" yelped Ava, "that is sooo rude."

He ignored her, fiddling with the focus until the binoculars gave him a really good view of Grandpa's beans and a moderately good view of Bella sniffing around a foxhole. He raised the binoculars in the direction of the harbour. He could see everything really clearly. An ice cream dropped by a toddler, a gardener locking up a goose, a patch of brambles with ripe blackberries, a really shiny bicycle. Further out a seagull shot across his vision. Resting his elbows on his knees he moved up over the undergrowth that surrounded the shore and past Thorn House's walled vegetable garden to swing over to the wilder woodland and the folly.

"Well?" asked Ava.

Josh didn't bother to answer. He'd finally reached his goal. One of the windows faced them and was blank, but the other had white squares on it. And there was a hand waving back and forth behind the squares. "H … E … L … P," he said. "Yup, HELP." He threw the binoculars up in the air and leaped from the bale. "ONWARD!" he shouted, charging back towards the farmyard. "Chloe's right. We have a mission!"

CHAPTER 5

"Wait!" yelled Chloe, stumbling off the bale and running after him.

"Let's rescue them ourselves," called Josh, dancing backwards into the farmyard, "with ammunition and a diversion and a giant cherry picker."

"That's a mad idea," replied Aiden.

"I don't see why not. It's obvious that no one believes us, so we have to do it ourselves." said Josh. "We could launch a full-scale attack – we could take the village tennis-ball machine and fire things at them. Like coconuts and … eggs." He looked at the others. They all stood with their mouths open as if he'd said the most stupid thing in the world. "Ugh! You lot. You're so boooring. You've got no…"

"Seriously?" said Chloe. "You're suggesting that we go in and free them? Ourselves?"

"We tried the harbour master," said Josh. "And then the pasty bobble-hat man rang the police – but you can see that nobody's *actually* done anything about it. The police are too busy to listen to anything *we* say. And even Grandma thought it was rubbish."

"I think," said Aiden. "I think…"

They all stared at him.

"I think…" He looked at Josh. "That Josh's almost possibly right."

"But who are we rescuing?" asked Chloe a few minutes later.

"Whoever's asking for help – silly," said Josh, beaming. "You said it yourself: Charlie's Cheerful whatsits," and he launched into song. "*Charlie, Charlie, love your doooog!*"

"Shut up, Josh – you are so jumping to conclusions here," said Ava, addressing them all. "It's probably nothing to do with the Cheerful Chew thing. I bet Grandma's right. And, the idea of us rescuing anybody from that tower is – idiotic."

No one answered her. They all stopped and looked out towards the island.

"I suppose," said Aiden in the end, "we just have to think of a way of getting them out of the tower and off the island."

"Aiden?" Ava pleaded.

"We could smuggle them out on the ferry," said Josh. "In a wheelbarrow maybe."

"Seriously?" said Ava. "You are seriously going to go over to an island and rescue an invisible person from a tower with a wheelbarrow?"

"I suppose a ladder might reach that window," said Chloe. "If we could get one over there."

"I think," said Ava, "that you're all completely mad."

"Are we?" said Chloe, wondering if it *was* a stupid idea.

"If we could get a ladder down to the *Black Diamond*, we could get it across to the island that way; the boat's long enough," said Aiden, taking off his glasses and polishing them on his T-shirt. "What harm can it do? We're just taking a ladder to the island – taking a look. If there's no one there, then..."

Ava stood, open-mouthed. "I ... I..." she began, before closing her eyes and leaning against the gatepost.

Josh, Chloe and Aiden stood blinking together at the cobwebby darkness of Grandpa's storage barn and, as they stood, staring, shapes began to make sense in the gloom. Kayaks, lawnmowers, bicycles, random wheels. There were ancient cracked gas masks and paint masks. Solid paint brushes and half-empty paint pots. A pile of sacks, plastic. A pile of sacks, sacking.

Chloe sighed. "What?" she said. "Who needs all this stuff?"

Aiden glanced back at Ava who was sitting on a stone mushroom playing games on her phone. They needed Ava. Without her they couldn't get to the island.

And she was the oldest.

The bravest.

And it felt wrong doing things without her.

Bella trotted up to Aiden, wagging her tail. "There must be a ladder here somewhere," he said, mostly to Bella but a bit to Chloe who was staring into the tangle of stuff and looking like she wished she'd never mentioned it.

"I've found a diver's helmet!" shouted Josh, advancing into the muddle. "Oh, and an old sewing machine! And a pram! Give me a hand someone – this pram's really cool." He pushed the pram into the doorway and climbed in, sticking his thumb in his mouth. "Waaaa!" he cried, doing a baby impression.

Aiden groaned. "Hey, Josh – we're looking for a ladder. This is serious, you know."

This was mad. He glanced back at Ava. She was still playing a game. Keeping out of it all.

Getting bored, Josh leaped out of the pram to investigate more things in the darker corners of the barn.

Aiden began to search properly. One end was definitely agricultural, the other domestic. Also, someone had stowed all the tall things together.

"Just let me get this out," he said to no one in particular. A sheet of corrugated iron slid easily from the front of a pile of tall timbers, releasing a mass of wolf spiders.

"Yow!" he yelped, stepping back.

Chloe ran out of the barn, flapping her hands at the back of her neck as if they'd raced straight up to her hair.

Ava picked her feet up from the ground and continued to look at her screen. "Yeah," she said to no one in particular.

But Josh was trapped because the spiders headed for the shadows, and he was in the darkest part of the barn. "Yow!" he yelled, blundering backwards through a pile of sacking and tripping over something noisy and metal. He reached out to steady himself and caught on more sacking, releasing a stack of garden canes. The whole lot cascaded to the concrete floor in a mass of clanging and banging and spiders and mice and Josh's knees.

Chloe peered round the doorway.

Aiden held his breath.

Bella ran after an escaping mouse as Josh emerged from the muddle, his hand clutching a section of something slightly shiny. "Here, look what I've found."

Aiden pulled away the piece of sacking. "Ace!" he said. "A ladder. A folding one. Brilliant."

"Supper time," came a shout from the house. "Pizza!"

CHAPTER 6

Ava barely slept. She spent the night thinking it through. It was all utterly stupid. Josh was stupid for suggesting it, and the other two were stupid for going along with him. Chloe was right. They didn't know who they were rescuing, if indeed they were rescuing anybody. It might be the missing child from Charlie's Cheerful Chews, but then again it might not be. And if it was, why would anyone hide a kidnapped person in full sight of thousands of tourists? Well, almost full sight. Full sight with the right angle and a pair of binoculars. And the police might have been and rescued them, or the police might have been and found there was no one to rescue.

She sat up on her bed, clasping her arms round her knees.

But, on the other hand, being stroppy was starting to get wearing. She hated not getting on with Chloe and Aiden. She hated feeling like the killjoy. She wanted to have adventures. Proper ones. Just not stupid ones.

"And anyway, how are we going to get the stupid ladder down to the boat?" She said it out loud, and immediately clamped her hand over her mouth.

"Are you awake?" asked Chloe from the darkness.

"Sorry, yes," said Ava.

"We could use the pram."

"The pram?"

"The one Josh was sitting in yesterday before all the spiders ran out."

Ava got out of bed and pulled back the curtains. The sky was full of stars. They lit the countryside outside their window. The bales they'd been sitting on earlier showed as black monoliths against a much paler field. She looked towards the old barn.

Its doors were open, but the inside was dark. The pram must be just inside the entrance.

She sighed. "I suppose it might work. Especially now we've got a folding ladder."

"It probably would. I mean it definitely would," said Chloe. "Can you see the tower from there?" she asked.

Ava opened the window wide and craned out. "No – but I can see the lighthouse, and the light flashing across the trees." She gazed down into the farmyard's dark shadows. "It's a shame the police didn't come."

"I suppose we could call them from here. Ask them if they've done anything," said Chloe.

Ava watched as the distant woods lit up every minute and the light scudded over the bay, and she came to a decision. "I'll go and call them now."

"Really?"

But Ava didn't wait to answer; she pulled on her slippers and slipped out of the bedroom door. The stairs creaked, but not too much, and she tiptoed through to the kitchen before switching on any lights. Bella snored under the table.

Picking up the phone, she dialled the emergency

number. "Emergency services, which service do you require, Ambulance, Fire, Police or Coastguard?"

Her heart loud in her ears, Ava asked for *police* and waited while the line clicked.

Bella woke up, wandered over and began to lick her face. "Police?" said the voice on the other end. "Can I establish your location?"

Ava gave the farm's address, and then began to explain what they had seen. The more she explained, the less convincing she realised she sounded. The person on the other end asked some questions, Ava answered them and then there was a pause. Eventually the voice on the other end said, "Thank you very much for your call – we will endeavour to make a routine visit within the next twenty-four hours."

And the phone went dead.

Ava stared at the receiver and put it back in the cradle.

"Any luck?" asked Chloe, who was waiting on the landing, her arms clamped round her knees.

Ava shook her head and both of them sneaked back to their beds.

"I don't think they believed me," Ava said,

playing the phone call back over in her head. "So we're back to investigating ourselves."

"Ava," said Chloe quietly. "I might have been wrong – I mean, suppose we rush over tomorrow with our ladder and we find that they're storing costumes up there or something, and there's no one who needs rescuing? Or even that the police *have* been and rescued them this evening. I don't want to be an idiot."

"Don't worry," said Ava, sniffing the night smells of damp stubble and dewy farmyard that drifted up to the window and coming to a decision. "Whatever happens it's an adventure – and we might find Jake's boat. You never know."

"Thanks," said Chloe, pulling the duvet up over her shoulder. "Thanks." And she snuggled back down to sleep.

When Grandma finally clanged the old ship's bell for breakfast the girls were already dressed, already in possession of the pram and very hungry.

The scrambled eggs were bright yellow, the toast was thick and plentiful, and a bowl of Grandpa's marmalade sat in the centre of the table looking delicious. Aiden and Josh stumbled down the stairs in their pyjamas. Aiden stared at the girls, already dressed and shovelling in eggs. "Where've you…" he began, tilting his head and frowning at Ava's big smile, but Chloe held a finger over her lips and he dropped the question.

Chloe pointed at the phone, mimed dialling, and then pointed at Ava.

Aiden mimed a helmet.

Chloe nodded.

Aiden pointed at the ground, meaning *Are the police coming here?*

Chloe shook her head and put on a sad face, but then smiled and pointed at Ava and mimed a ladder.

Aiden wondered if that meant that Ava had come round to the idea of the rescue. From the way she was sitting and smiling and talking it looked as if she had.

Spreading butter on another piece of toast, Aiden ran through the operation in his head. They hadn't really worked out the details.

There was the ladder, the boat, landing…

…and then there was the small matter of how to

get someone out of the tower, assuming that they were being guarded. It struck him that it was all very well lugging the ladder down to the boat and taking it across to the island, but how on earth were they going to get whoever it was out of the tower without anyone noticing? They'd need a diversion. A good one.

"Tea, anyone?" asked Grandma.

"Or apple juice?" said Aiden, standing up. He poured big glasses of Grandpa's cloudy apple juice for everyone. "Have you got any ketchup, Grandma?" Aiden asked, checking one of the cupboards over the kettle. "Please."

"Here," said Grandma, reaching into a cupboard above the dishwasher and handing him a mostly empty bottle of ketchup.

"Thank you," said Aiden, squeezing the tiniest penny on to the side of his plate and gently slipping the bottle down by his leg and holding it between his feet.

Josh did a caterpillar thing with his eyebrows and Aiden gave him a nudge.

"Blue skies," said Chloe, filling the silence.

"Yes," said Ava, springing up and pulling the

kitchen curtains right back to let in the sunlight.

"So what are you all going to do today?" asked Grandpa, slathering marmalade on a piece of toast and biting off the corner.

"If we can take the *Black Diamond* again, we're going to go on searching for Jake's boat on the island," said Aiden. "It's got to be there somewhere. Maybe it's on the other side."

"Definitely," agreed Chloe.

"Yeah," said Josh, "And we're going to find it and we're going to find out who's in the—"

"Tea shop on the island this year," finished Ava, sliding back to her chair and delivering a seriously hard kick under the table.

"Ow!" he said, scowling.

Grandpa stared from each cousin to the next and then smiled. "Jolly good, jolly good. Well, whatever it is you're doing, keep safe. Don't do anything I wouldn't do – you know, that sort of thing." He ran his finger through a stray blob of marmalade on his plate. "Hmmm." He glanced at Aiden and Ava. "Keep inshore. Don't want to call out the air-sea rescue." He laughed, although his eyes stayed serious. "Your grandmother and I are going over the moor later on to pick up five new hens, so I've made you sandwiches and you can always pop home if you're hungry." He started tidying plates into the dishwasher.

Chairs scraped as they rose from the table. Aiden slipped the ketchup bottle up under his T-shirt and tried to help Grandpa clear the debris of eggy plates and toast crumbs.

"Go on," said Grandma, "we'll do that. Off you go now, enjoy yourselves."

CHAPTER 7

While Chloe and Aiden strapped the ladder on to the pram with two crab lines and a kite string, Ava told them about ringing the police, and Aiden explained his plan. Josh tried to persuade a woodlouse to curl up.

"Yay! Aiden," said Ava, examining the knots holding the ladder down. "That's brilliant – if it works. So," she said, "you'll cross with me in the boat, and Chloe and Josh will take the ferry?"

"They'll have to," said Aiden. "They need the bikes for a quick getaway – and there's no way we can take bikes over on the *Black Diamond*." He pulled open the bike-shed door and disappeared inside.

"Yippee!" said Josh. "I love the ferry."

"Josh," barked Ava. "Behave – you're going to have to do what Chloe says. It's important."

"I will," said Josh, taking his bike from Aiden. He clambered on to the saddle and cycled in a tight circle, only slightly bumping into his sister. "I always do what I'm told."

"And I'm Beyoncé," sighed Ava, leaning down to lash the homemade ladder trolley to the back of her bike. Ava stepped over the crossbar and pedalled across the yard. The bike wobbled a little but the pram stayed fairly steady.

They set off in a sedate convoy, but within seconds Josh had lost patience and hurtled off ahead down the hill.

Chloe held back for a moment and then let go of the brakes, allowing her bike to follow Josh's and almost catch it before she lost her nerve on the bend and had to slow down. The bike's brakes juddered and she put her foot down to help a steep swing, pushing off from the bank and scaring herself by shooting down through the high hedges and whizzing past the sleepy bees to catch up with her cousin. She nearly caught him at the entrance of the village, her front wheel practically touching his rear wheel.

"Ha!" Josh laughed, turning his head and just missing a cat as it scuttled across the road. "Last one there buys the ice creams!" He swung to the right, dropping down a flight of steps, and this time Chloe plummeted down behind him, her teeth crashing against each other and her bike helmet slipping down over one eye until they bounced out into a square of fishy cobbles. Josh slammed on his brakes, and Chloe just missed him and a small child carrying an ice cream. Taking the scarily narrow route round a pile of nets, she passed him at the last second to stop behind the net-hanging shed, panting and spluttering.

"So you're buying the ice creams?" she said, giggling as she tried to get her breath back, her arms draped over the handlebars. "Mine's a strawberry split."

"Hello there," said a voice behind her.

Chloe couldn't help herself, she jumped. It was

Mr Bobble Hat from the café.

"Didn't mean to make you jump," he said. "Just wanted to tell you that the police came last night and went over to the island."

Josh stopped and turned. "Really? When?"

The man shook his head. "I've no idea – I was cleaning up. Let me think." He gazed up at a small white cloud as if it might tell him. "Must have been five o'clock at least. Could have been six. Long shadows, though."

"Do you know if they found anything?" asked Chloe.

The man shook his head. "No idea, I'm afraid. But they definitely went to look." He smiled. "Bye now, back to work."

Chloe and Josh stared as the man went back to the café and took up his place behind the hatch.

Josh raised his eyebrow.

The man waved.

"What do you think?" said Josh quietly.

"I don't know what to think," replied Chloe.

They both stared at the ferry queue, which was steadily growing.

"Well, I think we should do it anyway," said Josh.

"I mean, for all we know they didn't look in the right place. And it must have been at least eight o'clock when we went out to look from the field – there was definitely someone there then."

"Are you sure?"

"Yes," said Josh, pulling out his notebook and checking. "Yes. I am sure. Says here it was eight fourteen when we went back to the farmhouse. I'm going to stick to the plan. See you in a minute." He pushed his bike out into the open to join the end of the ferry queue.

A man with a Dalmatian dog joined the queue behind him.

Dalmatian. Where had she heard that before?

Chloe waited in the shade, watching the harbour fill with visitors. She just wasn't sure. Perhaps they should abandon it. She watched as a bus rattled down the hill and stopped next to the Plaice and Ships. Mr Bobble Hat served people ice creams, and she noticed how badly he put the gloop into the cones. Like someone not used to doing it. Several families filled the square, buying tickets and taking photos. Pearl was getting people into kayaks from the harbour steps. Jake was heaving lobster pots into a pile behind the pub.

A family stood in front of Josh and the woman ruffled Josh's hair. He swiped at her hand but still managed to look charming. Chloe knew he hated the ruffling thing. But somehow people found it irresistible.

Taking a deep breath, she wandered forward to join him in the queue. She tried to look like someone enjoying the sun. She closed her eyes and let the morning sunlight play on her eyelids. The world was bright red for a moment before she heard the rattle and squeak of Ava's bike.

The pram was still attached. And the ladder was still attached to the pram, but Ava was sweating and breathing hard. Aiden followed with Bella in the bike basket, his brakes squealing. A few people turned to stare, watching as Ava struggled with the pram bike convoy through a gap in the nets that was too small. No sooner had Ava rammed the bike through the nets than the pram hooked itself on to a stack of lobster pots and Ava stopped.

Bella leaped from the basket and began to bark at the lobster pots. People in the queue pointed and laughed.

Aiden leaned his bike against the heap of nets so that he could help Ava but the bike rolled backwards, subsiding in a spinning heap.

"Look at them," said a small child.

"It's rude to stare," said his mother.

Chloe turned away. Behind them the man with the Dalmatian was also staring at Ava and Aiden, and trying to get a signal on his phone.

"It won't work," she said. "There's no signal here; no signal anywhere around here."

He glared at her. "I don't need your help, little girl."

"Sorry," Chloe said, feeling a blush rise from her chest to smother her face.

The man turned his back, then glared across at Ava and Aiden struggling with the bikes. The dog sniffed at Chloe's hand, but the man yanked on the lead, pulling it away until it let out a little whimper.

He had a heavy face, lumpy and oddly sunburned. He wasn't local and he didn't look like a tourist. And he wasn't very nice to animals.

Her heart began to beat faster. She searched the rest of the harbour. Was anyone else interested in Ava and Aiden?

There was the man who'd been cleaning the outboard motor for a start; he was just leaning and staring, unsmiling.

She gripped the handlebars of her bike a little tighter and swallowed.

CHAPTER 8

In the stern of the boat Aiden felt himself blush. He hated drawing attention to himself, and all that stuff with the pram wasn't quite how he'd imagined it. He'd thought they would just slip on board the *Black Diamond* unnoticed and now they'd managed to attract the attention of the entire harbour and, to make it worse, there were seagulls circling over the boat and Bella wouldn't stop barking. And the ladder didn't really fit. It was squashing his toes and he knew that when Ava wanted the boat to change direction it was going to get difficult.

It was all getting very complicated.

Aiden watched Josh and Chloe get on the ferry. They were soon surrounded by a large group of cyclists. Then some families boarded and a few single people. One of them with a Dalmatian.

"Oh no," he said.

"What?" asked Ava, looking up.

"There's a Dalmatian getting on the ferry. I can't see if it's with the same man."

She crouched alongside Aiden and followed the direction of his pointing finger.

Aiden glanced down at his phone. He could warn Chloe but there was no signal. Of course there was no signal.

"But he might have nothing to do with it. He might just be a bad driver," she said, untying the painter rope. "And he doesn't know who Chloe and Josh are, right?"

Letting out a long sigh, Aiden muttered, "I hope you're right."

He watched as Chloe pushed through the crowds on the open deck of the ferry to stand by the rails at the side and saw her raise her hand in a tiny wave. He lifted one hand in reply.

"Right," said Ava, stepping over the oar and clambering past the ladder to the tiller. "We're off."

Aiden buckled his life jacket and settled on the bench. Early this morning this had seemed a really good idea. Sail to the island, take the ladder, climb the tower, free the prisoner or not free the prisoner, depending on whether or not they existed. Take them away, if they did. Easy.

But now…

He shuffled his feet under the edge of the ladder, watching the ferry as it sped towards the island. A small column of smoke trailed from the exhaust stack and the distant hubbub of chattering tourists floated over the water. He could no longer see Chloe, just a patchwork of colours and whirling seagulls as they followed the boat.

A slight breeze filled the sail and the dinghy slipped silently forward from the quay. Aiden looked around. There was hardly anyone to see them leave. Almost everyone had caught the ferry. There was only a tabby cat basking in the sun by the bins.

And Mr Bobble Hat in the Plaice and Ships café.

And the man they'd seen the day before cleaning

the outboard motor.

And Pearl.

And Jake.

Aiden watched them watching the ferry. He raised his phone to take a picture, but a lorry pulled into the harbour and blocked his view. Grabbing the map, he took out Grandpa's waterproof marker pen and, hoping Grandpa wouldn't mind, scribbled a quick picture of what he could remember. Big nose, bobble hat, weird toothy smile. Ordinary, fair hair, outboard motor. Pearl. Jake.

As a method of identifying anyone it was almost useless.

Ava steered them out of the harbour and into the open water. As they left the shelter of the harbour the sea broke into tiny blue-brown wavelets, streaks of shimmering colour racing left to right. A cormorant flapped lazily across the bay and a family of Canada geese argued over something under the water, but Aiden was too preoccupied to enjoy the sight. Instead he kept on glancing up at the lighthouse, staring at the tower and scouring the coast ahead for any sign of activity. His gaze flicked back to the café. Mr Bobble Hat had gone and

Aiden's mind ticked over. If the man in the queue with the Dalmatian was the same man that they'd met going to the lighthouse, was he anything to do with the possible kidnap? Was he working alone? If he wasn't, how many were they up against?

In his mind he began to put together a gang. Someone holding the boy in the tower. Dalmatian Man. Maybe the outboard-motor man. Probably others.

By the time they were nearing the island the ferry had disappeared behind the trees that sheltered the island's landing, and suddenly Aiden felt really anxious about his younger cousins attempting anything. Let alone his suggested diversion.

"Ready about," yelled Ava, and Aiden ducked under the boom, scrambling over the ladder and clutching the jib rope.

"I'm going to try to dock up to the right there – there's a broken jetty." Ava pointed to a dark patch between the trees. They sped towards the tower almost hidden in the tangle of branches and roots that marked the shore.

"OK," said Aiden, swallowing his anxiety. He took the mooring rope in his hand and clambered on to the bow. "I'm ready – take us in."

CHAPTER 9

Meanwhile, on the ferry, Chloe and Josh had made friends with three little dogs and bought a ninety-nine between the two of them. It wasn't a strawberry split and Josh didn't pay for all of it. There was no way he was actually going to buy her an ice cream. No one seriously expected you to keep promises like that – did they? Overall he thought that they were blending in very effectively, although Chloe kept patting her backpack as if she was carrying the Crown Jewels or something. He knew she was checking for the ketchup but even so, considering they were undercover, it was a bit obvious.

The ferry bumped on to the slope of the landing slipway and everyone streamed off: half of them went straight to the café, the rest milled around making decisions and giving Josh and Chloe the perfect cover. But soon a string of cyclists left and suddenly there weren't so many people in the open harbour. Josh leaned his bike against a bollard and swung a somersault round the metal barrier.

"Stop it," Chloe hissed. "We're supposed to be invisible."

"Huh," said Josh, using the topside of his trainers to brake against the paving. "You're only six months older than me, you know."

Chloe didn't reply; instead she used her bike as a weapon and shepherded Josh towards a big map of the island.

"But I know where the—" Josh began.

"Shhh," she said, waving at the map, picking out all the features, the tower included, but also the outdoor theatre and the dressing-up shed, and the ice-cream stall. "We don't want to be too obvious," she muttered. "We don't know who any of these people are." She waved her arm in a circle to take in the last of the stragglers from the ferry. Josh surveyed the leftover people.

"I see what you mean," he said, getting out his notebook and writing a few pithy descriptions.

Man with suit (odd).

Woman in floral-print dress with large earrings (odd).

Child with two ice creams (odd and greedy).

Two men in high-vis jackets (always suspicious).

Two women making phone calls (doubly odd when there's no signal).

One man with dog. Dalmatian.

The Dalmatian had been in the queue behind them.

He nudged Chloe. "D'you see that?"

She nodded her head and sneaked her hand into her pocket to pull out her phone. She hummed a couple of bars of a song and took a quick selfie, then turned her back on Dalmatian Man and took two more. The man barely glanced at them.

Good.

"Yes," said Josh to no one, noting in his book that the man's ferocious curly eyebrows met in the middle and that he walked with a roll, like Grandpa Winston.

Josh turned his back on the man and leaned against the Thorn Island map so that Chloe could go on taking photos. The man pulled on the dog's lead and wandered their way.

Chloe bit her lip and suddenly found something really interesting on her bike bars, but Josh wasn't a bit worried. It was just a man and a dog. He strolled over and reached for the dog's collar. The dog licked his hand, but the man jerked the lead, snatching the dog away. "Get off – this is a pedigree dog. Doesn't want some sad kid hanging around."

"Oh," said Josh, "I just thought he looked like he wanted a stroke." Persisting, Josh rubbed the dog's ears until the man grabbed the dog's collar and dragged it away over the gravel.

"Naff off," he barked.

Josh stepped back, hands raised, as the man and dog headed round past the café towards the Thorn Island Coastal Path.

"Josh," hissed Chloe when he had disappeared. "What was that about?"

"I wanted to find out if he was a nice man," said

Josh, staring towards the path.

"And?"

"He wasn't. He wasn't very nice at all, and that path is the one that goes towards the tower, isn't it?"

Very slowly Chloe nodded, and Josh noticed that she was gripping the handlebars so tightly that her fingers had gone white.

CHAPTER 10

"We should have gone the other way," said Josh, bumping his tyre into the back of Chloe's bike.

Chloe jammed on her brakes and Josh just avoided crashing into the back of her. "Sometimes, Josh, I really, really wish you'd just shut up."

Josh laughed, and then they pedalled on in almost silence, just the sound of seagulls and the soft hiss of the bike tyres on the woodland floor.

"Shh," Chloe said, braking with the soles of her trainers. She glanced at her phone again. Still no signal. She really wanted to warn the other two about the man with the dog. She looked out to sea. There was no sign of the *Black Diamond* – they must be behind the trees. Really close by.

"Look," said Josh. "The tower." Through the dappled shade of the leaves, the grey stones and slates of the tower were now really near. From this close it was even more magical. With a pointy slate roof and leaded windowpanes it looked exactly like something from a fairy tale and, from the side they were on, totally innocent. Next to it were two sheds and a door that Chloe assumed would be the way in.

She checked the time and looked out to sea again. Still no sign of the *Black Diamond.*

"I reckon they're already there," said Josh. "C'mon, let's get this done."

Chloe swung her backpack down to the ground and fumbled about for the ketchup bottle. It was plastic and squeezy and the ketchup was a little watery.

"Don't think they use it much," said Josh. "Give it a shake."

Holding the lid down, Chloe shook the bottle until the red coated the sides. "Come here then."

"Hang on," Josh said, and dropped to his knees, scraping through the leaf mould and summer mud. He straightened up and looked down at his legs. They were bitty and grubby and striped with gunk.

"Excellent," said Chloe. "Definitely makes it more realistic. OK, time for some gore."

Josh watched as she carefully blobbed the ketchup all around his knee and let it dribble down to his sock. Some of it was thick and some of it was thin.

"Quite like blood," she said, standing back and tilting her head to examine her artistry.

"Not bad," he replied. "Maybe stick a bit of gravel on it? I'vc ncvcr had a really good knee skid without gravelly bits getting stuck in."

"Good idea." Chloe took a handful of grit and splatted it on to the ketchup. She ran across the clearing and then turned back to take a look. From a distance it totally worked. "Try limping," she said.

Josh hobbled along the path, round a tall oak and back again.

Chloe watched as his limp changed from one side to the other. "Um, you need to make sure it's the same leg each time."

"I'll stick something lumpy in my sock. That'll

work." He sat on the ground and pulled off his trainer and sock. Chloe handed him two beechnut cases. "Ace," he said, putting his sock and trainer back on. He tried limping again. This time it wasn't too terrible.

Chloe checked the clock on her phone again. "Right, five minutes until we go."

"Let's go now, why wait?" said Josh, swinging his leg over his bike.

"No! They won't be—" said Chloe, but Josh was gone, pedalling towards the tower, then he threw himself from the bike and opened his mouth. The howl that he let rip made even Chloe jump – and she was expecting it. "Awwwwwwwowwwwwwww! I'm dead!" Josh shouted. "My leg! Awww!"

Furious with him, Chloe pedalled over, then dropped her bike and rushed to his side. She'd have liked to kick him but instead she said, extra loudly, "Are you all right? Oh!" She shouted towards the tower. "All that blood!"

"Argh!" yelled Josh. "Chloe – do something! I'm bleeding to death. Honestly – I'm all blood. It's blood gushing from my leg! I'm a bloody thing!"

"I'll go for help!" she shouted, although with

quite a large laugh. "Oh, look, maybe we can get a plaster in the tower!"

Feeling like someone in a pantomime, Chloe pushed through the last few metres of the path and stopped by the tower, Josh and his theatrical leg staggering behind her. They both took their bikes. Just in case. Before she knocked, Chloe looked again towards the sea. There was no sign of the dinghy – that would be because they'd started five minutes too soon. Josh was such an idiot! But she'd have to knock now. Any longer and the whole thing would fall apart.

But if the dinghy didn't come, then there wasn't a plan B.

Now she was closer she could see that there were two doors. She didn't know which one to knock on, but she imagined herself as someone with a person who had had an horrific accident.

She knocked on both.

On the other side of the tower Ava and Aiden were still bringing the *Black Diamond* into the shallow waters.

The ladder lay folded at Aiden's feet, but now

they were getting closer it looked as if it was going to be too short. As the boat slowed they heard Josh's terrible howl and shouting.

"What?" hissed Aiden. "But it's not even time. S'posed to be twelve o'clock."

Bella leaped on to the bow and let out a little growl.

Ava dropped anchor. "Bet it was Josh. I knew he wouldn't stick to the plan."

Thinking dark thoughts about Josh, Aiden dropped into the shallow water, his feet sinking into cold mud, as he grabbed the ladder from the boat.

More noise came from the other side: Josh's howls becoming more theatrical, which was when Bella decided to join in, howling and barking and finally leaping from the boat and charging past Aiden's legs towards the familiar voices.

"No! Bella, come back!" he yelled, but Bella had already disappeared.

"Forget her," hissed Ava, and together they ran forward with the ladder, extending it until the top was resting a metre below the high window. With a furious look on her face, Ava began to climb. The ladder sank very slightly into the soft mud. It creaked and made strange twanging sounds but it held firm, and Ava rose quickly past the lower windows until she was at the top. From where Aiden stood it seemed that the top of the ladder was definitely too low, that there was quite a gap between the top rung and the window ledge. It might be too big to make the ladder useful. He hoped he was wrong.

CHAPTER 11

When he opened the door Dalmatian Man was taller than Chloe remembered and heavier. Massive actually. He stood in the doorway and another man appeared behind him. He was also tall, but this man was leaner and somehow scarier. He was wearing a red vest and flexing his muscles like someone who worked out a lot.

Chloe attempted her sweetest smile. "My cousin's fallen off his bike – can you help? We can't get a phone signal," she added, looking past the men into the tower and seeing only a concrete floor and the Dalmatian. "Nice dog," she said rather quietly. "Your dog?"

Dalmatian Man just stared at her.

"Yes, dog. No, can't help," said Red Vest, spitting just past Chloe's foot.

"Hey," said Dalmatian Man, pointing at Josh who was now lying on the ground clutching at his knee. "Aren't you that kid I saw earlier – hassling Sandra here?" He pointed at the dog who raised itself from the concrete floor and padded to the door, licking a splodge of tomato ketchup from Chloe's hand.

"I dunno!" wailed Josh from behind Chloe. "Help!"

The ketchup had slipped down Josh's leg a little, looking more like he'd bashed his shin. Josh howled again and Bella burst out of the bushes galloping round and round in circles and barking madly.

"That dog with you?" said the man, starting to close the door.

"Please," said Chloe, stepping forward. "He's really badly hurt." Now that Bella was here she knew the *Black Diamond* was behind the tower, but the Dalmatian ran out to bark at Bella and followed her as she charged round the back and into a rhododendron bush that hid the creek behind.

"What's going on?" said Red Vest. "Something's going on." Shoving Chloe out of the way he clambered over the bikes and tried to follow the dogs but he couldn't get through the rhododendron's branches. Chloe wanted to run now, but she knew that every second they managed to slow down the men was a second longer for Ava and Aiden. Reaching for the handlebars she picked up the bikes and set them rolling so that they shot off in different directions, tripping Dalmatian Man.

"Oh dear," she said. "I'm sorry."

Bella shot back out of the bushes, ran in a barking circle and charged back towards the creek.

"This is…" Red Vest wrenched himself free from the rhododendron and took the dogs' path underneath. "Hey!" he shouted.

A woman's voice came from inside the tower. "What's all the racket?"

"Don't worry about us. Sorry to bother you," said Chloe, dragging her bike out from under Dalmatian Man and swinging her leg over the crossbar. "We'll find a warden somewhere. They'll have a first-aid kit in the café. Thanks anyway."

Dalmatian Man regained his feet and lunged towards Josh, grabbing his elbow.

"No you don't!" said Josh, sinking his teeth into the man's wrist.

"Ow!" shouted Dalmatian Man, clutching at his wrist. "You little—"

It took about a millisecond for Josh to scramble on to his bike, all thought of the gashed knee forgotten. "Yeah, I'm fine, actually," he said. "We'll be on our way. Thanks for your help." He pushed off and headed away, swinging and swaying towards Thorn Harbour, bumping at Chloe's wheel and speeding past her across the woodland floor.

"Hey!" shouted Dalmatian Man.

"The little toerags – after them!" shouted the woman.

But they didn't turn round; they just pedalled harder.

CHAPTER 12

As quietly as she could Ava tapped on the glass.

"Hello?" she whispered.

The window in front of her opened and a small boy's tear-stained face peeked over the sill. "Hello – are you help?"

"Yes," said Ava. "Are you the Charlie's Cheerful Chews boy?"

The boy nodded. "George," he said.

"Could you climb out, George?" It was about then that the two dogs appeared round the side of the tower. Ava glanced down. "Like, really quickly."

"I-I think so," said George, looking over the ledge.

"Ava!" hissed Aiden from below. "Hurry." As if Bella agreed she began to bark again, and louder.

"Now would be good," said Ava.

George sat on the windowsill and swung his legs over, leaving his feet dangling half a metre above the top rung of the ladder.

"Whoops," said Ava, trying not to panic at the huge gap between his feet and the ladder. She folded her arms across the top, making another rung. "Use me. Come on."

"Oh," said George, swinging round so that his armpits hooked over the windowsill, and his legs hung down as far as Ava's arms. His sandals rested on her elbow and wrist and she carefully took her other hand and guided his foot down to the top rung.

"I'm gonna—" he began, his voice wobbling.

"No, you're not, you're fine, come on," she said, getting his other foot down to the top rung. "Grab the top – we're going to have to speed up here."

"It's…" he said, bending double, balanced at the very top of the ladder. "I don't like heights."

Holding his calves steady, Ava tried to keep her voice cheerful and careless. "It'll be fine." Cries of pain came through the trees. She hoped they didn't belong to Chloe and Josh.

As George started to climb down the ladder a man in a red vest broke through the undergrowth, but Aiden was ready with a handful of mud, which he flung into his face. The red-vested man staggered to one side, but didn't fall over. Making it to the bottom, Ava and George ran past him and skimmed over the mud towards the *Black Diamond*. Bellowing, the man turned to follow them, but sank ankle-deep. He made an attempt at grabbing Aiden, but Aiden was now armed with a branch of rhododendron. He threw it into the man's legs, flooring him, and sending him face first into the sucky shallows.

"Yay!" yelled Ava.

"Aaawrgh!" the man shouted, pushing himself up out of the gloop like some kind of dripping mud monster. Standing, he blundered around blindly, crashing into the ladder and bringing it down on his own head.

Ava glanced back at Aiden. She was almost at the

boat, but the man wasn't giving up. Aiden needed to do something fast. And then George stopped.

"Hurry up!" Ava grabbed his hand and waded deeper into the creek, half leading, half dragging him. "Come on, we'll have you safe in just a—"

"It's cold!" said George, stopping with one foot submerged as large tears rolled down his face. "I want my mum, and I don't want to go into the cold water with *you*."

"Please just follow her, George!" shouted Aiden, reaching for a rotting branch.

"It's fine – just pretend you're at the seaside," said Ava, desperately tugging George's hand. "See –" she scooped up a handful of water – "it's the sea. It's really clear; it's just the leaves making it look black."

George almost looked as if he was going to trust her, when there was more uproar in the bushes by the tower. Bella burst through with a second man behind her.

"Oh no," muttered Aiden.

But Bella seemed to electrify George, and as she leaped for the *Black Diamond* so did he, grabbing her muddy fur and holding her tight. Ava followed, throwing herself over the side. "We're there!" she yelled.

Aiden was too far from the boat to jump in.

"They're going to run away without you," taunted the man in the red vest.

"You won't make it," said the big man behind him. Dalmatian Man. "Better give up now."

Aiden didn't answer.

Ava closed her hand round the tiller, willing Aiden closer.

At the last second Aiden threw the rotting branch at Red Vest's legs and ran. Splashing towards the *Black Diamond*, he launched himself at the side of the boat, pushing it out of the shallows, out of the shade of the trees to clear water where the sail could pick up a breeze.

He half swam, half waded, his glasses getting wet as he shoved the boat out of the shallows.

"C'mon – nearly there!" shouted Ava, just as Dalmatian Man managed to close his fingers round Aiden's trainer.

CHAPTER 13

"Faster!" yelled Josh as they struggled over the lumpy, bumpy roots of the trees.

Behind them he could hear shouting.

"Those two … tricked us … stop them!" He couldn't make out any more words, but the voice sounded very angry. Josh thought it was probably Red Vest.

"I'm on it!" came the woman's voice, and then he heard an engine. It might have been a strimmer, but he had a feeling it was probably a motorbike and that it was probably chasing them.

"They're going to be faster than us," shouted Chloe, swinging past an overhanging branch.

"I've got an idea," said Josh, desperately trying to remember the exact layout of the island. "Stay with me."

He swung to the right, shooting out of the trees and striking out across grassy parkland. There was no cover, just the occasional massive tree, but he could see the edge of the lawns of Thorn House and the thing Grandma called a ha-ha, which separated the formal garden from the rest of the grass. It was like a giant step about a metre high, with the garden above and the field below. The sheep in the park couldn't get up it. But he hoped he and Chloe could.

Behind them the motorbike burst from the trees. It was a hundred metres away, seventy, fifty.

"This is mad!" shouted Chloe. "We should head for the gate."

"No!" Josh yelled over his shoulder. "Trust me."

He made it to the ha-ha first, throwing himself off his bike and chucking it up into the garden. He hauled himself up on to the grass and grabbed Chloe's bike, dragging it up. Chloe followed a millisecond later as the motorbike thundered towards them. "Quick!" shouted Josh and he ran for the tall yew hedges that surrounded the flower beds, rolling his bike with him into the crowds of holidaymakers "ooohing" and "aaahing" over the floral displays.

Chloe remounted and cycled straight past him into the ornamental garden.

"You can't bring bikes in here," said a woman pushing a pram. "You have to go on the designated trails, don't they, Trevor?"

Her husband looked up from the guidebook and nodded. "Hmm, 'spec' so," he said, pointing at a piece of wall. "Henry the Eighth had that built, you know."

"Sorry," muttered Josh, desperately trying to keep Chloe in sight. Fixing a smile on his face he dismounted and pushed the bike through the crowds, bouncing the wheel on and off the paths, stopping and starting and bumping and braking.

"Ow!"

"Mind out!"

"You should be on the cycle path!"

"Sorry, sorry, sorry," Josh smiled, as sweetly as

he could, and attempted to look casual as he ran alongside his bike, trying to catch up with Chloe. Ahead of him she stopped to catch her breath.

"Come on," hissed Josh, hurrying past her. "We can't stop." He led the way through to the back of the garden, past the ornamental ponds. They bumped into more people and forced their bike tyres over more sandalled feet. Chloe must have said "sorry" a hundred times.

Josh resisted the temptation to look back; he was sure they were still being pursued. The motorbike wouldn't have been able to make it on to the ha-ha but the rider would.

He didn't want to slow down one bit.

Just as they burst out into the last section of garden, Josh heard a cry. "Hey! Kids!" It was the woman. He recognised her voice and he couldn't help turning round.

"Don't!" hissed Chloe.

"Stop, kids!" Josh saw the woman for the first time. She was wearing black-leather biker gear and looked out of place in the flowery garden.

"Look, your mum wants you," said an elderly lady feeding squishy banana to a baby in a pushchair.

"She sounds ever so upset."

"She's not our mum," said Chloe, pushing ahead until they were almost round the house, almost level with the drive. "She's a stranger – she's trying to kidnap us!"

"Kids!" Leather Woman shouted once more, this time much closer.

"Hang on a minute there," said the elderly lady, standing up and blocking the path. "You can't chase children that aren't yours."

"They're lying; I'm their nanny," shouted Leather Woman.

"She's not our nanny," yelled Josh, accidentally turning his front wheel and rolling off the turf on to a flowerbed and into a rose bush. Thorns from the rose dug deep into Josh's shorts. "Ow!" he squawked.

"Oh no!" Chloe dropped her bike on the grass and helped him tug but it seemed that the harder they pulled, the tighter the rose held on.

"Kids – is this woman your nanny?" asked a man with a toddler in tow.

"No – never seen her before today," said Josh, grabbing the thorny branch with his hand and yanking it from his leg. Something went ping and the rose sprang back, releasing him.

"What are their names then? If you're their nanny?" asked the man.

"Come on," hissed Chloe, whisking her bike from the grass and running forward with it on to the gravel of the drive.

Josh didn't need to be told twice. He put one foot on the nearside pedal, copying the old men he'd seen on bikes in the harbour, and got the bike rolling forward before he slung his leg over the saddle.

"Sasha a-and Calvin," Leather Woman was shouting, lunging forward. "And they're little horrors."

But by the time she'd persuaded the man with the toddler and reached the drive, Chloe and Josh were both freewheeling down the hill towards Thorn Island's harbour, the wind in their hair and their hearts landing back in their chests.

CHAPTER 14

Aiden launched himself across thc water. His fingers touched the side of the boat. He tried to grab it, but he was pulled backwards by Dalmatian Man.

Above him Ava wielded an oar, holding it like a baseball bat. "You can do it!" she yelled.

"Stop!" Dalmatian Man gripped Aiden's trainer while Aiden kicked against him.

"Aaargh!" screamed Aiden, giving another massive kick. He caught the man under the chin, making him stagger backwards, although he still gripped the trainer. Aiden fell forward.

"Go away, you horrible man!" shouted George, and he flung one of his sandals at him. It struck Dalmatian Man on his cheek.

"Yay!" shouted Ava.

"You little rat!" roared the man, stopping for a second to touch his face. It was just long enough for Aiden to wriggle his foot out of the trainer and splash into deeper water.

Aiden's fingers locked over the side of the boat and he worked his way round to the front, where he found the white snake line of the painter. "Yes! Paddle, Ava," he panted. Holding the rope between his teeth, he half swam, half drowned, all the while dragging the *Black Diamond* out to sea. He knew they had to get the boat out on to the open water before the sails would work and they could properly escape.

Aiden turned on to his back and kicked. Looking back towards the shore he could see Dalmatian Man hesitating at the edge of the deep water, still clutching his trainer. Then George threw his other sandal, catching the big man on the ear, and both of the dogs barked furiously.

"We'll find you and get you!" shouted the man, now armpit deep in the water, grabbing George's sandals and throwing them back at the boat. Ava ignored him, paddling hard with the oar as Aiden pulled the rope taut, and gradually they dragged the *Black Diamond* into clear sea.

The red-vested man shouted to Dalmatian Man and began to run along the shoreline away from them. Briefly Aiden wondered why.

Almost immediately a little puff of wind caught the mainsail and the *Black Diamond* overtook Aiden. With the calm skill that had impressed their grandparents, Ava manoeuvred the dinghy in a tight circle round Aiden.

"Gimme a hand," he said, throwing himself and his soggy clothes over the side of the boat. George grabbed Aiden's T-shirt and pulled until he could scramble over the top.

Aiden lay staring at the sky, water streaming off his clothes, sucking in lungfuls of air.

"Phew!" said George as he helped Aiden tug off his remaining trainer and got himself soaked at the same time. "Thanks," he said. "Thank you for rescuing me! I'm..." Big tears welled up in his eyes and Aiden reached across to hold his hand.

"That's OK. All in a day's work! Isn't it, Ava?" He tried to sound really cheerful, even though his heart was hammering in his chest and he was still shocked at what they'd done.

The boy wiped his eyes with the back of his hand. "George," he said. "I'm George Constantinides."

"Of Charlie's Cheerful Chews?" asked Aiden.

The boy nodded his lip, still quivering.

"I'm Aiden," said Aiden. "And that's Ava." He took off his glasses and wiped off the water on the bottom of Ava's T-shirt, which was still dry, and placed them back on his nose and then looked down at his soaking-wet clothes. Now that they were out of harm's way all the tension came to the surface, and a huge uncontrolled giggling snort came out of his chest. It was followed by another and another and he realised that he couldn't stop laughing, finding himself rocking backwards and forwards in the boat unable to speak. "Sorry! I just can't help thinking of the look on that man's face when my trainer came off in his hand. It was ace!"

Ava laughed too; like Aiden it surprised her, and it was a hiccupping kind of a laugh that came from deep inside. "Oh, Aiden, that was amazing!"

"We've done it!" cried Aiden, fighting his sopping-wet jeans, and peeling them down his legs. "We've freed you, and we're halfway home."

"Yes – but look!" said George, pointing back to a creek just beyond the one they'd left.

Ava turned to look. "Oh!" she said. "Oh no!"

CHAPTER 15

The cream-and-blue motorboat had twice the speed of the *Black Diamond*. Ava willed the dinghy forward as Aiden took the paddle and held it ready to defend them. As the motorboat approached their pursuers became clearer. There were two of them. Red Vest and Dalmatian Man. Both wet. Both angry. Ava glanced across at the oar. It wasn't much of a weapon, but with any luck Aiden would be able to pitch at least one of them into the sea. That just left one.

Ava shook the laughter out of her head. "So

there's these two, the big guy and the man in the red vest – who else?"

"I think there are four," said George, biting his lip. "They're the scary ones." He pointed at the boat. "The man in the red vest has a really bad temper. But there's this woman too. She was the one who took me – I was at my gym class – and there's another man."

"Tell us about the other man." Aiden put one foot on the bow of the boat and raised the oar. "What does he look like?"

"He's not at the tower much. He came over last night, but not this morning." George sat up and stared into space as if clearing his thoughts. "Don't know what he looks like – ordinary I suppose. They're all big, like really tall, and they eat a lot of chips."

"Chips?" said Ava. "Everyone eats chips round here."

"And pasties," said George. "They fed me on pasties. Cold ones."

"So the fourth man brings food?" asked Aiden. He bent his knees and took an experimental swipe with the paddle.

"Hold on," said Ava, pulling the sail tighter and sailing as close to the wind as she could. The gap between the dinghy and the motorboat was getting smaller second by second. They were starting to have to shout because of the roar of the motorboat's engine.

Bella left the bottom of the boat and put two paws on the stern, barking at the men behind and growling each time they lunged forward.

Without Bella, George hid himself below the bench, pulling his knees into his chest. Aiden glanced up at Ava and pointed at him.

"Hey, George, look in the forward locker," shouted Ava. "There'll be things to throw in there."

George rose to his knees and crawled under Aiden's knee to the enormous locker in front of the mast. There were apples and flip-flops. He armed himself, jamming the flip-flops down the top of his shorts and keeping an apple in each hand.

"We need more speed," said Ava. "Aiden, can you..."

Aiden abandoned the paddle and perched up on the side of the dinghy, leaning out backwards so that the back of his head almost touched the water as Ava pulled in the sail.

"What are you doing?" asked George.

"He's trying to keep us flat," explained Ava. "The more the wind tips the boat, the slower it goes. So we lean out to keep it level. Some of the big yachts have steel cables round them for people to lean right out."

The boy nodded. "Dad's yacht's got that."

"Your dad's got a yacht?" asked Ava. She couldn't actually think of anything better than sailing one of those big ocean-going yachts – with cabins and white tops and a proper crew. If only they had one right now, they'd easily outrun the motorboat.

It was now so close she could see it clearly. It was Jake's; it had to be. Brand new, blue and cream.

Aiden scrabbled in the rear locker and found a small life jacket. "Here, you might need this." He put it over George's head and threaded the lace through the holes. George looked slightly happier. Ava just hoped he wouldn't need it.

Ava took the *Black Diamond* away from the harbour and round the side of the island. She was taking a chance. They'd be out of sight of the shore and it would be more dangerous if they capsized, but there was more wind out at sea. They could go faster. The motorboat followed, turning messily, and bounced one of the men sideways.

"They're not wearing seat belts," said George. "They might fall out."

"Let's see what kind of sailors they are," Ava said, grasping the tiller firmly and leaning forward so that she could see under the sail. "Hold tight – we could end up getting wet." She swung the dinghy again, cutting a huge arc across the sparkling water and taking them right round the back of the island. The motorboat slowed, the driver obviously confused. He wrenched the wheel round and revved the engine.

"Yes!" yelped Ava, and she threw the dinghy back the other way, cutting a curve towards the island, again confusing the motorboat driver and creating a little space between the two boats.

But it didn't last long. The man in charge of the motorboat slowed, turned and pursued again.

This time Ava headed straight for the open sea, the motorboat almost reaching them, getting so close that they could see Dalmatian Man's wet clothing. "Duck," shouted Ava, and at the last second she jerked the tiller across the boat and reversed direction. The sail flopped and then instantly filled with wind, whisking them back towards the harbour, tilting the dinghy as they skimmed over the wavelets.

"Yay!" shouted George.

Aiden switched sides to level the boat.

But the motorboat recovered.

"Faster," shouted Aiden to Ava, and she hauled in the sail until the *Black Diamond* was leaning almost sideways in the water. Ava nodded her head and Aiden and George rushed to level her out, but the motorboat was still gaining.

"I'm gonna have to..." Aiden stood, wobbling towards the stern of the boat, paddle in hand.

Three metres, two metres. Red Vest stood, stepping forward on to the prow of the boat.

"Argh," shouted Aiden, slashing out with the paddle.

"No!" yelled Red Vest, trying to grab the end of the paddle and pull it.

Aiden held tight and shoved it at his belly. The man fell back and the motorboat rammed into the stern of the *Black Diamond*. Aiden slipped and fell into the bottom of the boat.

"Arrrgh," shouted George, wobbling to his feet and launching an apple at Dalmatian Man's head. The man let go of the wheel and the motorboat slowed.

The *Black Diamond* whipped forward, and George shot over the side into the water.

CHAPTER 16

"No!" yelled Aiden. Beneath him the water was glassy clear and still, and below that ridged sand caught in the fractured sunlight. It was so clear it was impossible to tell how deep it was. He threw off his glasses and plunged in, the bubbles racing past his ears. He didn't wait for them to stop; instead he reached his arms out, hoping to find George's legs.

He burst through the surface, right behind George.

"Help!" shouted George, spluttering and spitting. "Can't swim!"

Above him, the white blob of Bella raced along the *Black Diamond*, barking madly.

"You're OK – you're wearing a life jacket," said Aiden, pulling George's collar and kicking out towards the boat.

Ava had swung the *Black Diamond* so that it blocked them from the motorboat. Aiden knew they only had seconds before they were hit again and he pushed forward, grabbing the side and launching George over the top. It was all horribly blurry, but he saw George grab the oar and throw it over the prow of the *Black Diamond*.

"No!" shouted Aiden, too late to stop George from losing their only oar.

"Ow! You little—" shouted one of the men.

"George!" yelled Ava. "Hold this, here." She handed him the tiller and helped Aiden scale the side.

The motorboat circled them, and Ava took the tiller back. Aiden fumbled about in the bottom of the boat for his glasses.

"Hold tight," she muttered, sending the *Black Diamond* straight towards the motorboat.

"We're gonna—" began Aiden.

But at the last moment the motorboat swung sideways, turning far too fast and tipping.

Aiden saw the red-vested man hit the water.

Dalmatian Man stopped the boat and ran to the back.

"Yay!" said Aiden as the *Black Diamond* cut gently out to sea, leaving them behind. "Let's get some distance on them."

"We might just make it into shore, but the wind's in the wrong direction," Ava said. "And the tide's going out – there might be nowhere to land."

"Could we go further out?"

"I'm not supposed to, but..." Ava shrugged and pointed the *Black Diamond* out of the bay.

Which is when the wind became a breeze.

And the *Black Diamond* slowed.

Ava tried pulling the sail in different directions, but it didn't make any difference; they were going nowhere fast.

They all watched as the red-vested man clambered back on Jake's boat. They were only a hundred metres off.

"We can't do anything," said Ava. "We're helpless."

The power boat headed towards them.

Ava watched as Aiden checked all the lockers, but all he found were some flags and a bucket.

"They're going to get us," he muttered. "Sorry, George. We may have made things worse."

Using the little breeze that there was, Ava turned the boat. She was facing the long line of rocks at Gull Rock, and she had an idea.

Somewhere here was a wreck. She'd seen it from the clifftop once. If she could just steer in…

"Ava, you're heading straight for those rocks," Aiden said from beside her.

"Yup," she said, her tongue between her teeth, all her senses running on overdrive.

"But we'll hit them."

"No we won't," she said. "I know the tide's going out but…"

The *Black Diamond* slowed, but it didn't stop completely.

"Keep her level," said Ava, not taking her eyes from the gap between the two largest rocks.

George and Aiden moved into position, both of them gripping the side of the boat.

Ava glanced back; the motorboat was following.

It wasn't going so fast this time, but it was definitely catching them. She could see a puzzled expression on Dalmatian Man's face.

The rocks were almost flanking them. "We'll lift the centreboard," muttered Ava.

The *Black Diamond* now had only a few centimetres of hull below the waterline.

"I can see a dead boat down there," said George, looking over the side.

"Exactly," said Ava.

They glided over the wreck, which was just below the surface and just below the bottom of the *Black Diamond*, then sped up as the wind whistling along the coast caught their sail.

Ava leaned forward and dropped the centreboard again.

The motorboat, which was deeper than the *Black Diamond*, followed, driving into the gap between the rocks. It juddered as it hit the wreck beneath the surface.

And it stopped.

Dalmatian Man stood up, peered over the side and did a face palm.

"Yes," said Aiden. "Yes. They're stuck on

the wreck! Genius!"

Ava let the sail of the *Black Diamond* drop, and they drifted slowly away from the rocks, over a deep sandy pool that lay in the mouth of the bay.

Exhausted, Aiden and Ava high-fived and sat back on the benches to watch.

Jake's boat was wedged, clearly stuck on the submerged wreck. They saw the red-vested man clamber out, swim between the rocks and climb up on to the shore. Dalmatian Man followed him.

"Have we won?" asked George. "Have they given up?"

"Well, they can't get us here," said Aiden.

They watched the two men scale the small cliff and disappear off along the coastal path, heading back in the direction of the lighthouse.

"No," said Ava. "Unless they've got another boat, they can't. Now would be a brilliant time to get George to the harbour. Oh! But … look at the tide."

The water had receded so much Thorn Island was emerging from the sea. Huge sandbanks had opened up and the island now seemed to fill most of the bay.

"Can we go round the far side?" asked Aiden, noticing how long the shadows were and wondering how much daylight was left.

"I think we're going to have to, whether we like it or not," said Ava, looking out to sea at the big tankers on the horizon. "The tide's taking us. And there's nothing I can do to stop it."

"I'm hungry, I need a wee," said George just as Aiden opened his mouth, "and I want to go home."

CHAPTER 17

She tried not to, but Chloe had begun to imagine all sorts of terrible things. That Aiden and Ava had been shipwrecked, that the gang had got hold of them, that the wind had swept them out to sea – although there was no wind and Ava was a brilliant sailor.

Everyone on the ferry had seen the boat chase, and Jake had alerted the coastguard. The motorboat had been found jammed on an old wreck but nobody had been arrested. Because nobody was there.

And then it began to get dark.

"But they're kidnappers," Chloe had said for the millionth time.

"Yes, dear," Pearl had said soothingly. "Well done for spotting Jake's boat."

And so it went.

The thing was, the other two still weren't back, and there was absolutely no sign of them.

Chloe thought about trying to tell the coastguard but Josh talked her out of it.

"She'll be fine – she's my sister – and she's got Aiden with her. They won't do anything stupid. And Grandpa will be really cross about them sailing out of the bay."

So they trailed back to the farm, arguing the whole way. Chloe was eaten up by the idea that they should tell someone, and Josh was brushing aside each worry as she raised it.

"Hello, hello!" Grandpa greeted them near the back door, clutching a torch. "Picking slugs out of the strawberries. Best done in the dark. Where have you all been then? I heard that there was a little excitement in the harbour."

"Yes," said Chloe. "There was. And we're

worried. I'm worried."

"Shhh," hissed Josh.

"Tell me," said Grandpa, pausing.

"No, we *are* worried. I am," Chloe almost shouted. This time Josh was not going to talk her out of it. "Aiden and Ava took the *Black Diamond* out, and they haven't come back."

"Oh," said Grandpa. "Oh dear. Come inside."

They followed him in, Josh muttering something behind her.

Chloe ignored him. She sat down at the kitchen table and Grandma and Grandpa sat opposite, paying attention.

"So you all went out together?" Grandpa asked.

"No," said Chloe. "We went to the island on the ferry to—" She stopped. She couldn't explain about the kidnapping again – anyway, she didn't actually know if they'd rescued George. All she actually knew was that they'd somehow upset whoever it was that had stolen Jake's boat. "Anyway, Aiden and Ava went over on the *Black Diamond*, and then they went further round the island, and Jake's boat was following them and then Jake's boat was found, but the *Black Diamond* wasn't there."

Grandma looked at her sideways. She knew Grandma knew she wasn't telling the whole truth and she didn't know what to do about it. But she was telling them the important thing. She was telling them about the *Black Diamond* – about Aiden and Ava, and about not coming back.

"Hmmm…" Grandpa sat back and thought. "So could they have gone out with the tide?" he said eventually.

"S'pose so," said Josh, sniffing the air. "S'pect they're just fine."

Chloe felt enormously relieved to have told Grandpa, but she wasn't sure what he could do about it.

Grandpa rubbed his chin and then stood up and walked to the bottom of the stairs. Grandma Primrose took his elbow and said something to him that Chloe couldn't hear.

"Yes, I think I'll call the coastguard from my study," he said in the end. "I've just made a rather splendid vegetable curry and it would be a terrible shame to waste it. Why don't you have some while I'm sorting this out?" He turned back towards the doorway.

As if it had ears, Josh's stomach groaned long and hard. Grandma smiled. "Come on then. I'll boil some rice, and then at least two of you have had a hot dinner."

Feeling sick and hungry at the same time, Chloe pulled open the cutlery drawer and laid a couple of places at the table. The kitchen smelled divine, all spicy and sweet. Within minutes Josh had ploughed through two mountains of rice and thick delicious curry and chutney and poppadoms and naan, all washed down with delicate yoghurt drinks that Grandma had whizzed up in the blender.

Chloe ate half of hers.

"Thank you for that. Yummy," said Josh, rubbing his stomach. "I feel like falling asleep now."

Grandma looked at him over her glasses. "'Fraid you can't – I think we'll be going out looking for your sister and the *Black Diamond*. With your keen eyes we'll want you watching from the cliffs. The *Black Diamond* doesn't have any lights, you see – it's not supposed to be sailed at night." She smiled. "Least of all by your sister."

Grandma's smile slipped, and Chloe saw for a second just how worried she really was.

CHAPTER 18

Except for a slim moon it was almost completely dark as the *Black Diamond* finally slid into the shallow waters of Brandy Cove. It was eerily quiet. The caves in the cliff side seemed blacker than ever – dark mouths that Ava knew contained nothing more than dead seagulls. Off to the right the harbour looked cosy and warm, coloured lights hanging in strings over the pub and the glow of a barbecue outside on the quay. But the cove had seemed a better idea than trying to get into the harbour because of the black rocks that lay outside the harbour entrance. Ava wasn't sure she'd be able to avoid them in the dark. But now they were at the cove she wondered if landing here was just madness. She watched as Aiden jumped down on to the shingle.

He must be exhausted. He'd towed them past the island, the tide so low that at times the centreboard had scraped on the sand below. Sometimes he'd waded, sometimes he'd swam.

"Can I go home now?" asked George. "I'm scared."

"It'll be OK," Aiden said.

It was tricky in such poor light, but they managed to truss the sail and undo all the little cleats without losing any small bits. Finally they took out the mast and, ten minutes later, the *Black Diamond* had become a flat dark object that they pushed over the shingle into the largest of the caves.

They cast around on the shore in search of seaweed to drape over the black shiny paint and soon even the torch on Aiden's phone couldn't spot her from the beach. The only thing that was really visible was Bella, who ran up and down like a white ghost dog, sniffing and sneezing, probably glad to be back on land.

"Phew," said Aiden. "Now we climb the cliff – if we go round by the lighthouse, we can get back to the farm and call the police from there."

"OK," said Ava, feeling the beach for small round pebbles and finding lots.

"What are you doing?" asked George.

"Loading up my pockets," said Ava. "Just in case."

"In case of what?" he asked, his eyes wide in the almost dark.

"The enemy."

There was a quiet scrunch as Aiden scooped half the beach into his jeans.

The path up the cliff was really quite possible by day, but much trickier by night. The tussocks of grass that acted as handholds seemed to have turned grey by moonlight and blended into the sandy footpath. Ava led the way, with George in the middle and Aiden at the back, and they moved very slowly.

"Shhh," said Ava, stopping when they were about three quarters of the way up.

Aiden listened. He couldn't hear anything.

"Car," whispered Ava. "That means they might be above us, up at the lighthouse," said Ava.

George was barely awake and very heavy to pull along. Aiden sighed – he was tired too, and the idea that the gang might be behind them on the island or above them at the lighthouse was exhausting. They waited, crouching in the dark, the sea breaking on the beach below them, the moon above.

They began again, one step at a time, breaking through a small patch of something prickly at the top. This time Aiden saw headlights. The headlights swung across the bushes, briefly illuminating Ava's face and then they stopped.

"What?" asked George.

"Van," breathed Ava.

"White?" asked Aiden.

"Can't see," she replied.

The headlights went off, and Aiden heard the door of the van slam. He crouched, listening to his heartbeat and George's breathing.

The light of the lighthouse swept past, skimming the top of Ava's head.

Then Aiden heard the footsteps. Close, crunching footsteps, a few metres away – in the direction of the lighthouse.

He held his breath.

George held his.

Ava probably held hers.

A woman's voice came out of the dark. "You're surrounded. Give us the boy."

George drew in a sharp breath, and Aiden heard legs wading through long grass or bushes.

Bella sprang, a white ball in the darkness that bounded towards the woman, barking and growling.

"Now," shouted Ava, and she reared up in front of Aiden, delivering the first pebble.

Aiden jumped up behind her and held George's head down with one hand while flinging a handful of gravel with the other.

"Ow!" screamed the woman.

Aiden heard Ava crashing through the undergrowth somewhere to his right. "This way," he yelled, grabbing George's hand and setting off through the bushes to the left, away from the village and farm and away from anything useful, but towards the woods. He ducked and dived and zigzagged, trying to follow the path and not hit the tall spiky bushes that blocked it time and time again.

George ran with him, keeping up surprisingly well.

The lighthouse beam swept past them again, showing everything in their path. Ava shouted something behind him, which might have been "See you at the place".

Aiden speeded up as he remembered what Ava meant. "Come on, George," he said.

"Fast, fast," George panted behind him. "I'm going fast."

The two of them hurtled along the coastal path, Aiden with one trainer on and one socked foot, George in bare feet, until the bushes stopped on the left, giving way to open grass, which meant they were nearly at the woods.

As they ran Aiden listened for Ava, but she definitely wasn't behind them.

"Stop," he said, listening for footsteps. But there weren't any. All he could hear was George, the sea and the sounds of the night. She'd definitely gone towards the village. And hopefully she'd taken the scary woman with her.

The lighthouse beam bounced through the bushes, showing the cliff edge and the trees to the right.

"Has she fallen in the sea?" asked George.

"Shhh. No," said Aiden, but below to their left the sea boiled in a huge sinkhole. The water slapped against the sides, booming and shaking the ground beneath their feet. It was a scary place by day, and potentially lethal by night.

He knew that between their feet and the sinkhole lay a few metres of bunny-shaved grass and a thin strand of rusty wire. There was nothing else to stop them falling over. Above to the right was the coppice, and he could see the familiar silhouette of a tall beech tree against the faint light of the sky.

"This is going to be an adventure," he whispered to George, "but if we manage it, we'll have you safely out of their reach and back with your mum and dad in no time."

George didn't reply and Aiden wondered if the little boy was too terrified to speak.

If he remembered rightly, there was a fence on the other side. They needed it if they were going to get past the next part of the path. Blindly he cast about to his right until his fingers fell on something at waist height. He ran his hand down the side to check. It had two strands of wire at the top and sheep fencing at the bottom and it crossed a bog. A seriously boggy bog, one that Josh had fallen into last summer and had been pulled out of with a rope that they had to get from the farm. He had been in there shouting for some time. It had been very funny. But that all seemed a million years ago now.

"So, put your feet in the holes of the lower bit of fencing and hold the top bit to steady yourself. One step at a time." He sent George first. It was hard to see, but he could feel the wires trembling, and hear the twang as George's foot moved from one hole to the next. Aiden followed. Halfway across, the lighthouse beam swept the landscape again, this time showing their hands clutching the wire and the blackness at their feet. In silence they crossed the ten metres of bog.

By the time they'd crossed, the beech tree was just visible, but more as a shadow than a silhouette. Aiden stepped back on to the firm ground. "Now we just need to find our meeting spot in the woods."

CHAPTER 19

Ava grabbed Bella and ran the other way. On purpose.

She knew she had to lead the woman away. She also knew that every minute the lighthouse would light the whole landscape like a search beam.

But Ava had run out of pebbles. And now she was wondering if it had been such a good idea to go it alone.

Every time the lighthouse beam crossed the landscape Ava threw herself to the ground. Every time it swung past, Ava ran on. Bella, on the other hand, raced back and forth across the path, catching the light from time to time and managing to seem like three dogs.

Below, to the right, the sea swashed on to the shingle of Brandy Cove and, Ava hoped, kept clear of the cave. The awful thought that the *Black Diamond*, Grandpa's pride and joy, could be swept out on to the rocks made her run faster.

But as she ran so did the woman behind her. Step for step.

Faster! thought Ava, picking up speed and risking a change in direction, away from the coastal path and across an open stretch of field. She sprinted as hard as she'd ever run. In the distance lights were appearing in the village. Up to the left the farmhouse had a light on in the kitchen, but it was a long way. She would have to stop for breath; she couldn't keep it up for much longer. Desperate for a rest, she paused behind a clump of thistles, listening and gulping air. She couldn't hear anyone, but that didn't mean they weren't following her.

Putting her fingers to her lips she let out a long whistle, which she hoped was very much like a screech owl.

A distant answer came: another screech owl or Josh?

She tried again – this time a double call.

And the double call came back. Definitely Josh.

Ahead of her Bella shot off up the hill and vanished into the dark. Ava followed, homing in on her brother's very poor imitation of an owl.

CHAPTER 20

"I'm scared," said George, following Aiden through the trees.

"Don't worry," Aiden said, trying to sound really normal. "We're fine – we just need a particular place."

In truth, he was nervous himself, but he wasn't going to let George down. It was a little scary in the coppice; the moonlight cast such deep shadows behind the trees. Things crunched under his socked foot, and they weren't all leaves and twigs. Something was snuffling over to their right. A hedgehog perhaps? Or something bigger? Also, the thing that worried him most was that "the place" seemed to have disappeared. Last summer they'd built a den, but now it wasn't there. Or he'd got it all wrong and he was in a different part of the woods. The problem was that it was dark when they'd begun running, and he'd never been one hundred per cent sure of where he was.

"Let's take a moment to get our bearings," he said, listening out for the sea and realising that he could no longer hear it. They were quite a long way into the woods then.

"OK." George moved closer to him. "Can I hold your hand?" he asked.

"Of course," said Aiden. He reached out in the darkness and felt George's small cold hand. "So, George," he said ridiculously cheerfully, "what we're looking for is a really big tree – bigger than all the others."

Aiden felt George twist round to look at the dark sky.

"But I can't see," he said. "It's too dark."

"Tell you what," Aiden said, "let's get to the field edge and maybe we can spot it from there. OK?"

Pushing through some scratchy undergrowth Aiden headed towards what he thought was a patch of moonlit grass. They broke through the scrub and stopped, just before they trod in what was actually a dew pond. "Whoops!" he said. "I might not…"

The lighthouse flashed again and he realised that it was no longer behind them, but firmly on their right. Somehow he'd gone astray. He tried to remember where the woods ended and the fields began, but although the map was perfectly clear in his head, the actual landscape appeared to have changed. This was frustrating – he ALWAYS knew where he was. Being lost was an utterly new experience.

"Are we lost?" asked George in a tiny voice.

"Not lost," said Aiden. "Just…"

He didn't finish his sentence. He didn't want to lie, but then he didn't want to scare the little boy any more than was needed and also he didn't really think he was lost, not really, so much as unsure.

"I think we need a plan."

"What plan?" George's voice sounded more scared than ever.

"Well…" Aiden reached into his pockets. He had a phone, with no signal, but a light – and some soggy mints. "What have you got in your pockets?"

He heard George's jeans rattle. "A marble, a 'lastic band, my stretchy reflector sleeve thing."

"What stretchy reflector thing is that?" asked Aiden.

"This." George pulled something out of his pocket. Aiden couldn't see it at first, but when the lighthouse beam swept across them George's hand flashed green.

"My mum makes me wear it when I go on my bicycle, but I don't go on my bicycle because I fell off, but it's really good if you pull it straight – you can use it to pick up beetles."

George handed it to Aiden. "A reflector strip? That's brilliant," said Aiden. "I'm sure we could use that." For a moment they stood in the owl-quiet dark while Aiden thought. "Let's see if we can find a tree to climb."

It took them ten minutes to find a large tree that had fallen at a gentle angle against another tree.

"Here," said Aiden, lifting George on to the

bottom of the sloping trunk. "Try climbing up here."

"I'm scared," said George. "I'm not allowed to climb trees."

"It's fine. Hold my hand," said Aiden, gripping George's damp paw.

"My mum says I can't. And I haven't got any shoes on."

"Oh," said Aiden, forming a dim view of George's mum. "Well, she's not here right now, and I want you to, and you don't need shoes, so…"

George made an odd sound, which Aiden decided was a yes and they walked up the trunk. George held tight to Aiden's hand, and with a little slipping and sliding, they clambered into the branches of the other, upright, tree.

Soon they were out of the complete darkness and, as they rose, Aiden began to make sense of the landscape. There was the lighthouse, in front of it the cliffs, and in the distance the village. To the right the cliff edge was marked by the black balloons of bushes, and beyond that the sea was almost completely dark, but with strips of silver and flecks of white where the moonlight fell on the water. A boat with a searchlight was combing the bay. Was it looking for them?

Perhaps they should have stayed at the bottom of the cliff.

At least he'd have had Ava with him.

"OK there, George?"

"Can we go to sleep up here? I'm tired."

"For five minutes," said Aiden.

He wondered if they were safe to let the lighthouse beam fall on George's reflective strip. He couldn't see anyone from the gang. He couldn't hear anyone. And he needed the others. He let the beam swing by twice, and then, on the third time, he held up the strip, waving it, hoping very much that his cousins, and only his cousins, were watching.

CHAPTER 21

Twenty minutes later, Aiden was higher in the branches. George was wedged in a V-shaped branch below him.

"It's all right, George," he said to the possibly sleeping bundle below him. "The others are coming." There were indeed people coming, but they were coming from the lighthouse. Someone was searching the undergrowth near the tiny car park, and another one shone a light over the fields.

They were coming closer.

"Where are you Ava?" he muttered.

Over to the left he thought he could see some movement along the lane behind the lighthouse, but his night vision was so poor he couldn't be sure.

George stirred below him. "I want my mum."

Aiden thought for a moment. "We're going to play a game. We're going to see if we can run really, really fast back towards the sea. What do you think – could you beat me there?"

There was a long silence and a sigh. "I s'pose so. But we've already done this once," whined George.

"I know, but sometimes to avoid being caught you have to do things that you've done before," whispered Aiden, really hoping that George's voice didn't travel too far.

They crept down from the tree into the undergrowth, and as fast as he dared, he led George back towards the cliff.

George stopped suddenly. "What's that?"

"Where?"

"There, by my foot."

Aiden looked down. "It's a glow-worm, George. They come out at night in the summer."

"Are they electric?" asked George far too loudly.

"No, they're photoluminescent beetles," replied

Aiden, realising that there would now be a string of questions that he didn't have time for and probably didn't know the answers to.

"Why are they called worms if they're beetles?"

"Because," said Aiden, desperately trying to find the path in the blackness. "Look, there's another one."

George crouched and reached out to pick it up.

"No – don't do that. They're precious and need to stay put."

"Oh," came George's disappointed reply.

There was shouting over by the lighthouse and it didn't sound much like his cousins. Scrambling back down the cliff seemed the best of their options. They might get the attention of that boat with the searchlight, but failing that they could hide in the cave. Even swim to Drake's Bay if necessary, but being trapped in the woods didn't feel safe anymore.

Crossing the bog the second time seemed to take forever.

"Can we stop, please?" said George. "My feet hurt."

Aiden only had one trainer and he remembered

that George had none. Feeling suddenly guilty, he hoisted George on to his back and carried him piggyback along the path.

They passed more glow-worms and the scent of wild honeysuckle.

Aiden paused and listened. The hillside was alive with sounds: crickets, snuffling things, owls, and now he could hear the sea pounding against the cliff at the bottom. It occurred to him that the tide might have come right in, in which case they wouldn't have a beach to go to. They'd be trapped on the footpath.

He crept on, George becoming heavier with every step.

Distantly a helicopter began to fly back and forth across the entrance to the bay. Aiden was glad it was so far away– the last thing they needed was to be lit up from the sky.

Crouching low, Aiden followed the path until they were right by the top of the cliff. Huge black bushes surrounded them – anyone could be hiding in them, but Aiden had no choice but to go forward. He looked around, wondering if his cousins would find them. Five would be better than two. You couldn't grab five children. Not easily.

"You're going to have to get down now," said Aiden. "I don't think I can go along the path carrying you."

George slipped round Aiden's back and landed softly on the nibbled grass. "Is this going to be scary?"

"It'll be fine," Aiden lied.

They'd gone about twenty metres down when Aiden heard someone crashing along the coastal path from the direction of the village.

"Quick! Down!" he hissed, pulling George under a blackthorn bush. It caught in Aiden's hair and his T-shirt and spiked him in the back, but he kept quiet and put his hand over George's mouth.

He held his breath and George held his, and they waited.

CHAPTER 22

The first pair of feet passed him and then the second, then a wet nose thrust its way into the bushes and started to lick his face.

"Bella!" exclaimed Aiden.

Josh screamed.

"Aiden?" said Ava. "Is that you?"

"Yes!" he said, laughing with relief as he struggled on to the path. "Me and George. Whoa – we're glad to see you."

"Phew!" said Chloe.

"I'm hungry," said George.

"I was trying to get back to the shore," said Aiden. "There's a boat down there with searchlights."

"Leather Woman's at the top of the cliff, though," said Chloe. "We had to crawl through the bushes to get here and Bella made such a racket, I don't think we can get past that way."

"We could run back into the woods," said Josh. "Build a fire – set up a diversion."

Aiden sighed. "We're too tired for any of that."

"We'll hide in the top cave," said Ava, heading over to what appeared to be a precipice.

"I'm tired. I'm going to sleep on this," said George to himself, patting an anthill, though no one was listening. "Or this," he said, prodding a tussock with his toe.

The others were silent, concentrating on picking their way through the lunar landscape of the moonlit cliff and down the perilous path on the other side. Twenty metres further down, Ava suddenly disappeared into deep shadow.

Josh paused and followed suit.

Chloe led George into the shadow and, bringing up the rear, Aiden checked that no one was following them before ducking and entering the blackness too.

Using her phone, Ava lit up the interior of the cave. On the floor lay a few smashed eggshells, and growing from the walls, samphire, but no dead seagulls, no dead fish and a platform of sandstone that was almost like a bench. It smelled of the sea and dripped like a sea cave, but they were well above the tideline.

"Wow!" said Josh. "I never knew this was here. How come you know about it, sis?"

"Grandma Primrose, wasn't it? When we were little?"

Aiden nodded and pointed at the ceiling. "She wanted to show us stalactites. See?"

Ava shone her phone at the long formations of rock hanging above their heads. The shadows were long and strange. Bella trotted to the mouth of the cave and sat down outside.

Aiden sagged to the bench and Chloe sat next to him, opening the backpack. "There's some curry in here. You two could share it," she said, handing the tub to Aiden.

"Grandpa Edward's curry? Oh, wow!" said Aiden, ripping off the lid and offering it to George.

"Food!" said George. "Who are you?"

"Chloe," said Chloe. "And you must be George." She handed him a cheese sandwich to eat alongside the curry.

"Aw, thanks, Chloe," said Aiden. "So what did you tell Grandma and Grandpa?"

"I told them that you and Ava were lost. They're looking for the *Black Diamond* – with the coastguard."

"Oh!" said Aiden. "That must be the helicopter then. Did they know Ava was back?"

Chloe shook her head. "Grandpa went with the coastguard, Grandma stayed at home in case either of you came back, and we were supposed to look along the coast – which is when we found Ava."

"I tried to stop her telling anyone," said Josh. "I was quite sure you had it sorted."

"I had to – you might have drifted out to sea and been lost forever," said Chloe.

"We nearly were," said Ava, stuffing a cheese sandwich in her mouth and following it with some chocolate.

"Who's that?" asked George, pointing at Josh.

"I'm Josh," said Josh, sitting on the other side of George. "Now, would you like crisps or a chocolate eclair?"

CHAPTER 23

When Josh woke a little before dawn he found his sister and Bella sitting on guard at the entrance of the cave – fast asleep.

He watched the light grow, the pitch black giving way to grey. Shapes emerged from the darkness and resolved into houses. The horizon appeared with the faintest hint of gold.

A bird began to sing somewhere in the scrub. Just because, Josh thought, it could.

He searched around for something to burn and found dried grass and twigs that had blown up into the cave, and he set about making a fire. It wasn't that he really needed the warmth and they didn't have anything to cook; it was just that to do the whole caveman thing he felt he needed a fire in a cave – even if all he had to roast was a dried apricot.

Next he set about making a spark. Except all he could find was limestone and sand, neither of which gave the slightest glint of fire. He tried to remember the other ways of making fire. A stick and a flat piece of wood. He could make a bow perhaps.

He left the cave and wandered up the path. It was still quite dark, and he was so intent on searching for the right kind of stick that he didn't realise how far he'd gone.

"Whoa." He stopped at the top of the path, just short of stepping out on to the cropped grass that surrounded the lighthouse. He dropped to all fours and was about to crawl back when he heard a voice.

It was Leather Woman. Talking to someone.

He crawled round a bush until he could almost see.

"They're here somewhere."

"What do you mean?" said a man's voice. Josh didn't know whose it was, but it didn't sound like Dalmatian Man or Red Vest.

"Nearby – really close," said the woman.

"There's no sign of them in the village. I'd know," said the man. "We could just make a run for it. Forget the whole thing."

"Too much money at stake. We'll get the boy – and get Stig to deal with the others. They're only kids."

"If you think so."

"I do."

Then there was silence before the woman spoke. "I've been out here all night – no one's been past, and I'd know. They have to be in those woods, or…"

Her voice faded. Josh risked lifting his head but he couldn't see anything.

So there really was no point in getting back along the cliff. They had to go down. Disappointed to discover that his sister was once again correct, he scuttled back down the path with a handful of possible fire-making twigs.

He grabbed a strand of old man's beard to be

the string and he set about making a fire bow.

Thweeeee, thweee, thewweeee. Thweeee, theweeee, thewweeeee.

The bow spun the twig round and back again, rubbing against the fence post below. He put his finger to the join. Warm. Definitely warm. So he tried again.

And again.

And again.

Five minutes later, the tiniest coil of smoke rose from the fence post.

"Yay!" he cried.

"What?" said Aiden, stumbling blearily to the mouth of the cave and seeing Josh crouching by his miniature fire. "You're mad! You'll bring them running."

"Really?" said Josh, pointing to the smouldering blade of dried grass. "It was just a small fire."

"Put it out," said his sister, rubbing her eyes and sitting up.

Sighing, Josh stood up and stamped on the small smoking curl of dry grass. "You're no fun. Anyway – I know something you don't."

"What?" she said.

"I know that that woman's at the top of the cliff waiting … and I've heard another man who wants to give it up and run away, but she won't let him. *She's* the leader. AND they said that Stig, whoever he is, is going to DEAL WITH US."

Ava stared at him.

"S'true, honest."

"Let's go," said Aiden, and he led the way through the gloom towards Brandy Cove.

CHAPTER 24

"What are they doing?" asked George.

Chloe held her finger up to her lip. "Shhh, George," she whispered. "They're checking to see if it's safe for us to go back to the boat."

George nodded and chewed his nails. "I'm hungry," he said. For a moment Chloe felt furious with him. Hungry, now, when they were risking everything to get him back to safety? But then she saw it from George's point of view. She wondered just how scary all this had been for him. Being kidnapped and then being dragged all over the place by first Ava and Aiden, then Aiden, and now all of them. He was only six. She gave him a hug and held him close.

Ava beckoned them forward.

Keeping George by her, Chloe sneaked over the long rocks and down the other side to the sea cave.

"Boat's here," said Ava, venturing into the cave first.

Chloe stopped behind her. It was so dark she could barely see the boat. Just the faintest grey outline.

"Help me move her to the water," said Ava, pulling at the stern.

The boat didn't move. Aiden joined her – but still the boat didn't move.

It took all of them pushing and pulling to get it to shift over the shingle, and in the half dark they stumbled and bumbled and it took an age.

By Chloe's feet Bella sniffed and growled at something under the dinghy.

"Weird. The boat seems to be much heavier than yesterday," said Ava as the sides creaked. "I hope we're not doing any damage."

Chloe hoped so too. Aside from what Grandpa

might say, there was the thought that five of them were about to set sail in the *Black Diamond*, and if she wasn't seaworthy it might be a very short voyage. She tried to lift as she pulled and Ava did the same and Aiden joined in, so the boat mostly slid, and sometimes bumped, to the shallows.

Aiden tied it to the stumps of an old jetty that stuck out from a rock and they all stomped back up the beach to rescue the mast.

"So," said Aiden as they bent down to pick it up, "we'll sail straight for Drake's Bay, put the *Black Diamond* in the boat shed, then form a guard round George and take him straight to the harbour master's office. Yes?"

"No," said Ava. "I'll bring her in where the ferry lands. It'll be easier to get George off safely."

"You are so wrong!" said Josh, waving his hands in his sister's face. "They'll be waiting for us. We should go to the boat shed."

"Stop it, Josh," said Ava. "Stop it. The boat shed'll be more dangerous."

George didn't say anything. He sat down on the shingle and found some apricots in Chloe's bag.

"They might be waiting for us in the boat shed,"

said Chloe in the end. "We'd be out of sight, so we wouldn't be able to do anything to stop them there. We need to be somewhere more public."

"Yes," said Ava. "Exactly."

Aiden examined the back of his hand; Josh dug a hole in the shingle with his heel. They glanced at each other and nodded. "OK."

Ava directed them as they re-erected the mast, lifting it into position.

"Wow," said George. "It's a sailing boat again."

Ava jumped aboard, helping George in. Josh scrambled in next, clutching Bella, and Chloe and Aiden pushed the boat so that it was no longer resting on the sand and was into deeper water. It seemed heavy, but then there were already three people on board.

"Will it take five?" asked Chloe as Ava took the tiller.

"George is only small," Ava answered, and then, as if realising that this was a little rude, added, "Sorry, George, but you are quite little."

George smiled and investigated the rear locker for the remains of yesterday's lunch. He found half a scone.

Aiden clambered over the side and Chloe stood knee-deep in the water ready to give the boat a final push. She glanced up at the cliff. There was no trace of anyone following them. But she felt uneasy. As if there might have been someone there watching.

"OK," said Ava, "put the jib up please, Josh. And give the boat a shove, Chloe."

CHAPTER 25

The dinghy began to move, rocking from side to side as Chloe was hauled on board. It felt very heavy and very low, and as she pulled the sail tighter and the boat began to tip Ava realised she had only a few centimetres of clearance before they would take on water. This would be a harder sail than she had ever done before.

"Keep her level, can you?" she said to the others. Chloe and Josh leaned out on the side, bringing the boat flat, but only for a moment before it began to tip the other way.

No one said anything. If they made it out of the cove without being spotted, it would be a miracle.

With the exception of Ava they all looked back towards the cliff, and as they travelled further out into open water their gaze went up towards the lighthouse and the scrub along the coastal path.

As if someone had opened the curtains light began to pour into the bay. Within a few minutes the vague dusky outlines of the boat became real and colourful.

With the sun came a more normal feeling. Surely nothing could go wrong now? They just had to make it into the harbour.

"Can you see anyone?" asked Ava.

"No one," dared Chloe.

Aiden nodded.

Distantly they heard an engine fire up, but it could have been from anywhere.

"How many cars did the gang have?" asked Aiden.

"They had a white van," said George.

"Right," said Ava, scanning Thorn Island as they cruised past. She couldn't see anything sinister, just an early-morning gardener pulling a wheelbarrow from a shed, a small rowing boat tying up at the quay, a window cleaner and someone sorting through recycling.

Three seagulls swooped over them and headed on towards Drake's Bay.

"It's taking ages," said Josh.

"There's a lot of us," replied Ava. "Lower in the water, more drag." But he was right; it was taking ages. The *Black Diamond* was sluggish despite a good wind and calm waters.

The first ferry of the day came out of Drake's Bay and headed towards Thorn Island. A red fishing boat left the harbour and headed out to the buoys that marked the lobster pots.

The wake from the ferry drifted towards them and they bounced over it, rocking unsteadily, water slopping over the sides.

A crow landed on the mast, Bella growled and it squawked and flew off.

"Come on, little boat," said Aiden. "Hurry up."

Ava noticed that he was staring back towards Brandy Cove. "Anyone on the cliff now?" she asked.

"Just seen a person looking out to sea. Might be a walker, though."

"S'OK," said Josh. "If they saw us now, they'd have no chance of getting to Drake's Bay before us. We're fine."

No one spoke. The only sounds were the gentle slapping of water on the bow and the distant hum of the harbour waking up.

"Rats," said Aiden, pointing up the cliff.

"What is it?" asked Josh.

"The van, the white van – it's coming down from the lighthouse."

"Oh!" said Ava, struggling with the tiller. The *Black Diamond* seemed to have a mind of her own this morning: first slow, now leaning to starboard. "Move to the other side, Josh; I think we're lopsided."

"All right?" asked Aiden.

Ava swallowed. "There's something wrong with the boat – she's really weird to steer."

"Perhaps it's the currents?" said Aiden, who was watching the white van winding through the village. "Look, there they are."

Two people emerged from the white van. From out at sea it looked like Leather Woman and Dalmatian Man.

"Wonder where the others are," muttered Aiden.

"We don't even know what one of them looks like," said Ava.

The buildings of the harbour were now quite clear.

"Two minutes," said Ava, pulling the tiller round and tightening the sail.

A coach pulled into the harbour. People got out and flooded the quay and headed towards the hotel.

The *Black Diamond* lurched round and slid sideways towards the open mouth of the harbour. Ava tried to correct the angle and the boat staggered to port.

"Are you going to be able to do this?" asked Aiden.

"Yup," said Ava, keeping her eyes on the scrap of old jetty to the right of the main harbour, right under the harbour master's window. "Gently does it." She pulled the tiller across as slowly as she could, keeping the boat upright and letting the sail sag so that they almost stopped.

Aiden stepped forward on to the bow and took the painter, ready to tie the boat safely.

Ava guided the dinghy the last few metres.

Aiden sprang to the quay, rope in hand. Ava let go of the tiller and began to furl the sail so that they weren't swept off again.

A pair of seagulls dive-bombed some chips dropped on the quay and in the confusion Ava almost didn't see the man climb out of the forward locker.

It was Red Vest and he went straight for George. "Gotcha!" he shouted.

"Chloe!" shouted Aiden.

But Chloe wasn't quick enough, nor Josh, and in one step Red Vest leaped on to the quayside, carrying George, and tried to break into a run.

Aiden dropped the rope and Ava tried to grab it, but suddenly there was Bobble Hat from the Plaice and Ships café racing towards them, his arms out.

"Don't panic!" he shouted, grabbing George and Red Vest.

For a second Ava relaxed, thinking it was all going to be OK, but then she heard George yell, "He's one of them!"

"What?" said Aiden. "I thought…"

As Ava, still standing in the boat, struggled to

find a weapon, Bella shot past her – leaping four-square at the two men.

"Aaargh!" shouted Mr Bobble Hat as Bella knocked him into Aiden, who had armed himself with a lobster pot and was swinging it wildly.

Red Vest moved out of the way, letting go of George just as Mr Bobble Hat crumpled on to the quay.

The little boy fell straight down the gap between the *Black Diamond* and the shore, and into the water.

"No!" gasped Josh.

"He can't swim!" shouted Aiden, still struggling with Red Vest.

Chloe kicked off her trainers and dived in over the side, the wake of bubbles eclipsing her and George completely.

Tourists began to arrive at the top of the quay steps, crowding around and getting in the way.

Bobble Hat sat back, clutching his arm, Bella standing guard, but Red Vest brushed Aiden aside and ran for the harbour steps as if he was going to dive in too. Aiden followed, raised the lobster pot and this time brought it down on the man's head.

Mr Bobble Hat jumped up in time to be grabbed by Jake and Pearl who had appeared through the crowd.

"DON'T YOU DARE!" shouted Pearl, pushing Mr Bobble Hat up the steps and yanking his elbows behind his back.

Chloe bobbed to the surface, George's collar in her hand, and pulled herself round to the stern of the *Black Diamond*. While Josh and Aiden pulled and Chloe pushed, George emerged, spluttering and blinking, from the water.

Ava found a spare length of rope in the rear locker. She made a noose and leaping on to the quay she ran round the back of Red Vest to throw it over his shoulders. "Yay!" she shouted, pulling it tight and trapping his arms at the elbow.

"What the devil's going on?" said the harbour master from the top of the steps, his face red with fury. "What are you kids doing?"

"Call the police," shouted Josh. "They're kidnappers – this is George. Of Charlie's Cheerful Chews."

Then Grandpa appeared at the top of the steps, beaming and then frowning as he looked down at the mayhem. "I say!" he said. "Jolly pleased to see you lot. But…"

"And there are two more of them in the white van in the harbour car park!" shouted Aiden. "Leather Woman and Dalmatian Man – someone needs to get to them fast, before they escape."

Grandpa and Jake didn't waste a second, running back to the car park, while the harbour master rushed back to his office to ring the police. Chloe and George climbed the steps and stood at the top, streaming water and laughing at Ava and Aiden sitting on their captive. Josh stepped into the harbour master's office to make sure that the harbour master got his facts right.

Ava saw Grandpa clamber in to his old Land Rover and park it across the top of the lane that led to the harbour, blocking everyone in, and Jake stood alongside, daring anyone to try and get past.

There would be no escape for Leather Woman and Dalmatian Man.

And no escape for the bedraggled man whose ankles Ava was securing with yet more knots.

CHAPTER 26

Later, sitting up at the table in the farmhouse, Ava could only marvel at the size of the hot chocolate she'd been given. It was truly incredible. Double marshmallows, double cream. And crisps.

"So," said the policewoman who had arrived with the marshmallows and crisps, "can I get this straight? The man who you caught and trussed was crammed into the forward locker all the way from Brandy Cove?"

Ava nodded and popped another marshmallow in her mouth. "Yup."

"He, I believe," said the policewoman, "is Stig."

"Suits him," said Josh, stealing a marshmallow from Ava's hot chocolate.

"The boat was behaving weirdly," said Aiden. "We were really slow all the way, really low in the water, and it must have been because he was jammed in there."

Grandpa, who was drinking a milkshake, raised his eyebrows.

"And then, when we moored—" interrupted Josh.

"He sprang out of nowhere—" butted in Chloe.

"And grabbed George," said Ava.

"Right from between us while we were looking at what was happening on the quay," said Chloe, dipping another chocolate biscuit into her milkshake.

"And then Aiden whacked him with the lobster pot," said Josh.

"I did." Aiden flushed. "Was that OK?"

"Needs must," said the policewoman, smiling.

"Did you?" said Grandma, sitting down and fanning herself. "I don't know how I'm going to tell your parents all this."

"Well, if he hadn't, then the man would have got George back and got him in the van and then we'd have lost him again," said Josh. "And that would have been really bad."

"Quite," agreed the policewoman. "It would."

"And then George would have been kidnapped again," said Josh.

"And we wouldn't have these heavenly milkshakes," said Chloe, licking her straw.

"No," said George, taking a sip from his milkshake and then dipping a biscuit in and finally taking two flakes and stuffing them in his mouth all at once. "And that would be a very bad thing." He beamed at them all and then pointed out of the window at a huge shiny black car that had just arrived. "MUM!"

CHAPTER 27

It was after the weekend when the invitation came to meet George and his parents and have lunch at Long House Hotel. None of the cousins had ever been there. Grandma made them brush their hair and wear clean T-shirts.

"Really?" said Josh, rubbing spit on yesterday's T-shirt, which to him didn't really seem to be too bad.

"Really," insisted Grandpa.

They piled into the Land Rover and bobbled through the lanes as Grandpa drove.

The big shiny car was there, and as they entered the garden George ran out from inside and threw his arms round Aiden's legs. "Yay!" he yelped. "So glad you're here – and you can order anything – Mum says."

They followed George inside and met his mum and dad, who were really smart and really nice, Chloe thought. For about five minutes everyone was very well behaved and extra polite, but gradually it became a homely mix of everyone talking over everyone and everyone eating and ordering and laughing. And having a good time.

They stayed long into the afternoon – and there was cake.

Afterwards they made friends with the five new hens that Grandma and Grandpa had brought home. They were all glossy and black, and so shiny that their feathers shone almost green in the sun.

One of the hens was smaller than all the others and struggled to keep up. She raced back and forth across the pen, but her legs were shorter and she had to try harder.

"I think," said Josh, picking her up, "that we should call this one George."

"George?" said Chloe, stroking the hen's head. "But she's a girl."

"So?" said Josh, putting the little hen back in the run next to the corn.

Later they climbed into the old apple tree, protected from the hot summer sun by its dappled leaf shade. From here they had an uninterrupted view of the still waters of Drake's Bay. Butterflies flitted around the flowers in the border, bees buzzed and the distant sounds of the harbour getting on with normal life floated up to them.

"That," said Chloe, "was properly scary."

"That," said Josh, "was properly an adventure."

"It had its moments," said Aiden. "I never want to hide in a tree again."

Ava gazed at the weathervane on the little tower over at Thorn Island as it caught the sunlight. She saw Jake's motorboat tied up in the harbour, the distant shingle beach at Brandy Cove and the twinkling waves lapping on the shore. She couldn't think of anything to say. Being at Clifftopper Farm, being with her cousins, being with her grandparents and having so much freedom. It was simply the best – thing – ever!

More Great Fiction From Nosy Crow

A Waterstones Book of the Month

"I adored this, a genuine feel-good delight with the most lovable animal narrator."

– Fiona Noble, *The Bookseller*